EARL OF
ST. SEVILLE

Wicked Earls' Club

Christina
McKnight

PRAISE FOR CHRISTINA MCKNIGHT'S NOVELS

THE THIEF STEALS HER EARL

"When I started reading this book I could not put it down...it caused another book-hangover for me. I wanted to see how things would go when the truth of Judith came out and how Simon was going to handle it...loved it."-*Sissy's Book Review*

"Jude and Cart's story is such a delight! So refreshing to see the hero shy, socially awkward and not super wealthy. I love it...This was definitely one of the best books I've read this summer." -*Reviews from a Thrifty Mom*

FORGOTTEN NO MORE

"This author has made me love historical romance again." -*TwinsieTalk Book Reviews*

HIDDEN NO MORE

"The storyline was really good, the writing was great. So smooth and engaging, I was able to zip right through the story, it flowed so well. I love finding new to me authors and with this wonderfully written by Ms. McKnight I've found a new historical romance author."-*Bound by Books*

CHRISTMAS EVER MORE

"*Christmas Ever More* was a wonderfully written festive novella full of hope, renewal, love, and new beginnings. If you're a fan of Christina's Lady Forsaken series, this is a must. Even if you aren't caught up, this stands well enough on its own to be a lovely addition to your holiday reading list."-*Literal Addiction*

BOOKS BY CHRISTINA MCKNIGHT

The Undaunted Debutantes Series
The Disappearance of Lady Edith
The Misfortune of Lady Lucianna
The Misadventures of Lady Ophelia

Lady Archer's Creed Series
Theodora
Georgina
Adeline
Josephine

Craven House Series
The Thief Steals Her Earl
The Mistress Enchants Her Marquis
The Madame Catches Her Duke
The Gambler Wagers Her Baron

A Lady Forsaken Series
Shunned No More
Forgotten No More
Scorned Ever More
Christmas Ever More
Hidden No More

Standalone Titles
The Siege of Lady Aloria, a de Wolfe Pack Novella
A Kiss at Christmastide
For the Love of a Widow
Earl of St. Seville
The Lady Loves a Scandal
Bound by the Christmastide Moon
Bedded Under the Christmastide Moon

DEDICATION

For my sister

ACKNOWLEDGMENTS

A VERY special thank you to all my WICKED EARLS' CLUB authors. We came, we saw, we conquered!

There are so many people who support my passion for writing. Here are a few I am blessed to call friend: Marc McGuire, Lauren Stewart, Erica Monroe, Amanda Mariel, Debbie Haston, Angie Stanton, Theresa Baer, Ava Stone, Roxanne Stellmacher, Laura Cummings, Dawn Borbon, Suzi Parker, Jennifer Vella, Brandi Johnson, and Latisha Kahn. Thank you all for accepting me for, well, me.

A very special thank you to my editor, Chelle Olson with Literally Addicted to Detail, your skill and professionalism surpass all that I expected. Chelle Olson can be contracted by email at literallyaddictedtodetail@yahoo.com.

Also, a special thanks to my developmental editor, Jessa Slade.

And to my proofreader, Anja, thank you for embarking on yet another journey with me.

Cover design and wraparound cover design credit to Sweet 'N Spicy Designs.

Finally, thank you for supporting indie authors.

PROLOGUE

January 1822
London, England

JAMES LANE, THE Earl of Desmond, strolled down the darkened lane bordering Covent Garden without benefit of the gaslights that were commonplace in the more civilized areas of London. Pall Mall, Oxford Street, Bond Street, and even Savile Row in Mayfair. The earl pulled at the lapel of his coat to keep the crisp evening air from sending wave after wave of shivers through him. He wasn't as young as he'd once been, nor was he as strong or confident as the young lord who'd claimed the love of Ivory Bess not far from this very spot.

The clip of horses' hooves sounded behind Desmond, reminding him that losing focus and letting his guard down in such a neighborhood—and so late into the night—could mean his death. He glanced over his shoulder. No one followed as he hurried toward his carriage, halted at the end of the street—only four dark and abandoned buildings away—his driver idly passing the time huddled in his thick, wool coat on his perch where Desmond had left him two hours prior. His footman kept watch near the boot of the carriage.

Despite his advanced age and the frigid January weather, the earl continued to visit London's more dubious neighborhoods.

Even with the love of his life taken from him five years ago, Desmond came. There was a day when he'd thought his life ended with her. His countess, the mother of his children, the love of his life was gone from him. However, Ivory "Bess" Lane, the Countess of Desmond, his wife and soul mate, had left a piece of herself in each of their children, Patience especially.

It was for his youngest daughter, Lady Patience Lane, that Desmond risked his safety night after night when he journeyed round London, entering various gaming hells and taverns.

If it weren't for Patience, Desmond would have retired to his country estate in Somerset to live out his days surrounded by things that reminded him of his Ivory—their many good years together before the trials of her youth came back to haunt her.

Yet, retiring to a life of solitude in the English countryside was not to be…

"More's the pity," he mumbled into the night.

Desmond would have his time to grieve once all his daughters were happily wed. His sons would find their own way, just as Desmond had after he left University.

Two down, and only Patience left unattached—sadly with no prospects on the horizon.

Shoving his gloved hands deep into his greatcoat pockets, his fingers wrapped around the newly printed pamphlets he'd come to Covent Gardens to distribute. He knew it was a lost cause, but it meant something to Patience.

Ironically, distributing Patience's precisely crafted pamphlets also decreased her chances of finding a suitable match even more.

The men—and many women—who gained their living stripped down to the waist with their bare knuckles raised and poised to fight were not interested in learning about the risks of their pugilist pursuits. Damnation, many of them couldn't so much as read the pamphlets Patience painstakingly created. They were not interested in the injuries and damage caused by repeated blows to the head and torso; they were more concerned with earning the coin to pay for food and shelter. A livelihood for themselves and their families.

Many in London had no other means but what could be gained by using their brute strength, sure fists, and light feet.

Be that as it may, he continued to indulge Patience. He'd never tell her that her hard work littered the floors of gaming hells as men readily discarded the papers as rubbish, or was used to wipe down grimy windows. She never journeyed to any of the hells and taverns and so never knew the fate of her pamphlets.

Desmond had slowed as he allowed his mind to wander.

Another sign he had become overly lax during his nighttime trips across London.

Keeping his eyes on his driver perched on the seat of his waiting coach, Desmond increased his pace, ready to escape to the solitude of his study.

With only two buildings separating him from that fate, the earl passed an alley littered with debris and spoiled table scraps—where two men could be seen embroiled in a scuffle.

He ought to avert his gaze and keep walking.

What transpired in the dark lane between two grown men was none of his business and could lead to Desmond being injured or even killed. It would do his children little good if he got himself stabbed for interfering in something that was not his concern.

Yet, he stared into the alley as the men tussled, knocking one another to the ground.

Haphazardly hung fabric in the windows of the tenements were pulled back as the people living above the alley stared down at the spectacle, the candlelight from their open windows casting a glow around the two men. Twenty years ago—perhaps as few as ten—Desmond wouldn't have hesitated to separate the two men before anyone was grievously injured.

But now, he had less time to live—and so much more he needed to see done before he left this life.

Another tenant in the building above pulled back what appeared to be undergarments strung on a line for drying, sending more muted light through the grimy windowpane and directly down on the skirmish below.

One of the men was outfitted as most were in the Covent Garden district: loose trousers and a long, hole-ridden tunic with shoes years past needing mending by a cobbler. However, the other opponent could not be mistaken for anything but gentry, if not a lord like Desmond. As the fighters regained their footing, the earl noticed that the nobleman's sheer size nearly filled the alley from stone wall to stone wall, his height as impressive as his stature. His hair, hanging past his shoulders in golden brown waves, was the only hint that mayhap he was not among London's elite *ton*, for what man—except highwaymen and pirates—allowed his hair to fall down his back at such a length? For a brief second, the light reflected off highly polished Hessians as the massive Corinthian sidestepped a fist, causing the smaller man to list forward and slam into the stone wall as his balance fled him.

"Come 'ere, ya toff," the man called, turning away from the building and raising his fists in preparation for another assault.

Desmond wasn't certain how the finely dressed man had wandered down this particular street, but a thief had obviously set upon him. Perhaps he'd been visiting one of the various gaming hells situated several streets over.

The ruffian threw another jab, catching the larger man in the mouth.

The gentleman needed assistance. Despite Desmond's age and frailty, he was the man's only option this far into the alley, no longer in view of Desmond's carriage and driver. If the earl screamed for help, would his driver come running? Desmond would never forgive himself if injury came to his servant as a direct result of his call for help.

Glancing around, Desmond spotted a long, wooden handle, likely discarded when the hammer portion broke from the end, making the tool useless except as fire kindling.

It would do the job needing done. He only needed to create enough of a distraction for the gentleman—and himself—to escape the alley and flee to the waiting coach.

Desmond took hold of the wooden rod and advanced farther into the dim alley as the ruffian, his trousers as threadbare as his tunic, swiftly jabbed his fist, pummeling the other man in the chest. The fighters shuffled their feet, clench fists raised as they hopped in a tight circle, each looking for another opportunity to strike out at the other.

It was a scene Desmond was all too familiar with.

The exact occurrence that Patience's painstakingly crafted pamphlets hoped to discourage.

Desmond inched closer and bided his time. He waited for the men to move so that he could club the lout with enough force to halt the attack. If Desmond struck at the correct time, he and the other gentleman could depart the alley without further confrontation.

Finally, the moment presented itself, and Desmond swung the thick stick with enough force to nick the man's shoulder and send him reeling to the muck-strewn dirt.

The Corinthian paused, his eyes darting to Desmond and back to his assailant as he moved to regain his feet.

"I think it best we leave," Desmond called, discarding the club against the alley wall out of reach of the ruffian, the sound echoing in the alley. "Let us be off."

When the gentleman made no move to follow him, Desmond wondered if he'd made a grave mistake by assuming that the henchman was the aggressor in the situation.

The smaller man regained his footing quicker than Desmond anticipated, though only grabbed the gentleman's coat where he'd discarded it on a stack of crates against the alley wall. He fled deeper into the dark passageway, disappearing from sight, his footfalls echoing in the wake of his escape.

Neither Desmond nor the other man moved in pursuit.

"My carriage is down the street," Desmond said, nodding toward the mouth of the alley. "Your lip is split and may need stitches to mend properly. Come, I will have my personal physician tend to your wounds."

"The chap stole my overcoat," the man breathed, his hands resting on his hips as he sucked air in deep, wincing slightly. The cut on his lip most certainly stung when the night air hit it.

Desmond wanted to chuckle. "At least you are escaping with your life and no new holes on your person."

He remembered being young and impulsive—exhilarated at the thought of a skilled match against an accomplished pugilist.

Again, Desmond wondered if the man needed saving to begin with.

In that moment, Patience came to mind; her single-minded determination to warn fighters about the peril they faced when they accepted the challenge of a worthy competitor. Lost memories, unending bouts of lethargy, headaches, and vision impairment.

His Ivory Bess, once a prized pugilist in her own right, had suffered more than most with all those ailments.

Desmond narrowed his glare at the man, tilting his chin up to focus on the gentleman's face and not his chest. "We should go, in case the man decides to return."

"I can find my own way back to my lodging."

"I'm not certain you even know where you are, my friend," Desmond retorted. The maze of alleyways and lanes that crisscrossed London were difficult to navigate, and even more daunting in the dark.

Candles extinguished as the residents of the building overlooking the alley lost interest in the scene below. With their departure, the meager light that had shone down on the filthy passageway disappeared, shrouding Desmond in shadows as unease rose the hairs on the back of his neck.

Desmond turned, waving for the man to follow. "My coach is this way."

Exiting the alleyway, the earl curved right and was reassured to see his coach and driver waiting. A sharp whistle garnered the driver's attention, and his servant leapt down from his perch and whisked the door open, not bothering to set down the steps.

Desmond took the forward-facing seat, surprised to note that the stranger alighted directly after him, taking the seat across from him.

"My townhouse," he called as his driver closed the door.

"Right away, my lord."

The carriage shifted, and the creak of the brake

lever broke the silence in the confined space as the horses were called into action.

"My lodging is at the Albany." The man's deep voice reverberated off the walls of the coach. "I will be forever grateful and in your debt if you can deposit me there."

He was definitely of noble birth, as further evidenced by his cultured tone.

Desmond scoffed. "There is no physician in residence near the Albany at this time of night. My doctor will see to your wounds, and I will arrange for transport back to the Albany after."

The grim set of the man's frown told Desmond that he was not used to answering to another.

That made two of them.

Besides his three hellion daughters, Desmond's edicts were taken as strict orders, and no one in his household disobeyed his command.

"Your name, my boy?" Desmond took in the almost unbelievable width of the man's shoulders and the sharp edge of his jawline. He was at least twenty years Desmond's junior, if not more. And the earl recognized the rebellious light in his eyes all too well.

Reluctantly, the man answered, "Sinclair Chambers—err, Earl of St. Seville. And who shall I commend as my guardian angel?"

"The Earl of Desmond, James to my closest friends." He eyed the man across from him, St. Seville's dark eyes appearing black in the dim interior of the coach. "St. Seville, you say. Of the Brownsea Island St. Sevilles?"

St. Seville's brooding mask of irritation transformed to utter shock. "Yes, you know of my family?"

"Your father is—err, *was*—Ellis Chambers?"

"Correct." St. Seville crossed his arms over his chest, and a new guarded mask hooded his expression.

"Were you acquainted?"

Desmond could barely believe his eyes. If he looked closely at the young man across from him, he noted the hardened jawline and severe nose with a mouth that appeared more of a slash across his face that was so characteristic of the St. Seville family, even with his split lip that now boasted a patch of drying red blood. Even if the man seated facing Desmond were twice the size of his predecessor, the earl could see the family resemblance as clear as if they stood under a bright June sun with the men side by side. Desmond hadn't seen the elder St. Seville in over two decades. He'd nearly forgotten the man's existence.

"Ellis and I were once close—both members of The Earls' Guild here in London—however, he left town shortly after his wedding and retired to his family estate. If you have taken the title, I assume your father has passed. When did it happen?"

"Going on four years now." St. Seville glanced at the window, pulling aside the cloth covering the glass insert. "My mother and sister remain on the island."

Four years, and word hadn't reached Desmond.

To be fair, his mind had been occupied with his own sorrows. Five long years since his wife had left him alone, and it was still all Desmond thought of.

"I am sorry for your loss," Desmond sighed. "Ellis was a good man."

A snort was the younger man's only reply as the carriage pulled to a halt.

"I can see myself back to the Albany and take care of my own needs, my lord." His gruff reply had Desmond wondering if he remembered Ellis incorrectly.

"I am afraid I must insist on seeing to your care. It is the least I can do for my old friend, your father." Desmond held St. Seville's weary glare as his driver opened the door to allow them exit. "We lost touch all those years ago, and I fear it was my duty to remain in contact. Please, allow my physician to see to your injuries. It would do much to assuage an old man's guilt."

Desmond saw the moment the man acquiesced; his stiff shoulders sagged a bit, and he nodded.

CHAPTER 1

THE FAMILIAR CREAK of a window opening in the room next door startled Lady Patience Lane from her deep slumber as a tremor of fear rolled through her. A chill ran up her spine despite the warmth of her room. Rubbing at her sleep-heavy eyes, she stretched her legs toward the cooled coals at the end of her bed as she sat up and listened. She tuned her hearing to any sound that did not belong.

Marsh Manor, the name her mother had christened their family townhouse with upon her marriage to her father, had been an unusually silent home in recent years. No longer did the structure ache and groan as it settled, no doors opened and closed in the night, and no windowpane was ever cracked during the bitter cold of winter despite the three other bordering buildings that blocked the worst of the late January wind.

Merit's room lay next door to Patience's, but the bedchamber had been empty for nearly two weeks, seeing that her brothers—Merit and Valor—had fled the dreary London weather for a holiday party near the Scottish border. Both of her sisters were happily wed and residing with their husbands, and they hardly visited unless her father commanded it. Besides her father and the Desmond servants, Patience was alone in the townhouse. Certainly, no servant had been tasked to clean Merit's room this late at night. The Desmond household didn't always stand on formalities, so when Patience and her father retired for the evening, so too did their staff.

When no other odd noises broke the silence of the night, Patience wondered if she hadn't imagined the entire thing and relaxed back into her soft, feather-filled bed. She pulled her covers high to her chin and closed her eyes, willing herself back to slumber.

Thump.

Patience sat bolt upright in bed, clutching her warm blankets to her chest as her wide-eyed stare darted around her dark room. The faint glow of the embers in her hearth told her that the hour was late, and the entire household was likely abed, despite the lingering warmth in her chambers.

Yet, *someone* was indeed in Merit's room.

Perhaps her brothers had returned early from their holiday.

The sound of a cough echoed through the thin wall, followed by a groan, and then another cough. An ensuing litany of cursing echoed, too low for Patience to comprehend every word but enough to fill her with a burst of happiness.

Her rascal of a brother *had* returned…and without the foresight of sending word to her.

Had he stopped at his club for a drink—or three—before arriving home? Perhaps that explained his less than subtle arrival and his string of highly unacceptable language.

None of that mattered. Her brother was home. Patience would no longer suffer through endless days of solitude with little conversation besides what she engaged in with her father or her maid.

Patience tossed her blankets aside and scurried from the sanctuary of her bed, her bare feet touching the cold, wood-planked floors as she hopped across the room in delight. Her unease from a few moments before was all but forgotten in her haste to chastise her brother for his untimely arrival, thus rousing her from sleep.

She wasn't actually vexed—quite the contrary in fact.

In truth, she missed her siblings greatly when they were not at home.

With her eldest sisters—Verity and Temperance—lovingly wed and living with their husbands, Patience found herself alone much of the time, her father hidden in his study claiming he had much work to do and could not be bothered by her idle chatter. Patience did not, in any way, see her discussions and debates regarding the health and safety of all her countrymen as idle *or* chatter. However, in addition to passing around her pamphlets, her father had begged her to set her attention on other topics.

That only left Valor and Merit to keep her company and banish the loneliness that had set in after their mother's passing five years prior.

Patience pulled her door open just enough to slip into the corridor, a draft ruffling the hem of her long, white nightshift around her bare ankles.

Indeed! A dim glow shone below her brother's door.

The eagerness that coursed through her was unexpected, though welcome. Except for her work crafting her pamphlets, Patience had little to occupy the long hours in each day, though she had taken her father's advice and researched drought in the Southern African nations and the extreme poverty currently plaguing areas in Eastern Asia. She suspected he'd only suggested the distraction to keep her mind occupied.

Visitors were few and far between at Marsh Manor. Any friends she'd thought to possess had long been married and now had their own families to care for and were, therefore, not concerned with the grave injustices around the world nor continuing a friendship with a woman who now verged on being a social outcast. At twenty years of age, Patience had danced her way through three Seasons before setting her sights on other activities to fill the endless days—far more noteworthy and pressing matters than what color was fashionable during the current Season or what lord every marriage-minded mum desired to set their caps on for their unattached daughters.

Not that she verbally admonished those who filled their every waking moment with such drivel—regularly, at least.

Her only reprieve from her causes was her rakehell brothers—and the mischief they found, even though they were both past the age of childish games. Her sisters, bless them, had both turned into tedious shells of their former selves, preferring to spend their time on the trivial matters of societal life, the exact things that Patience had, for lack of a better word, no *patience* for.

Patience took a few steps toward Merit's door before glancing across the hall to Valor's bedchambers. No light could be seen in the space between the bottom of the wood and the polished floor. Odd, her brothers never went anywhere without one another. They were joined at the hip, as her father liked to jest—thought Patience sometimes called the pair joined at the brain, as they seldom had any original thoughts between them.

But, as her sisters were always eager to remind her, it only mattered that a gentleman was pleasing to the eye—and heavy in the pockets.

Merit and Valor were most assuredly dashing young men with ample funds provided by Patience's father. She supposed a handsome exterior, large, deep pockets, and sense to use both wisely would be a rare combination indeed.

Patience grasped the latch to Merit's door and pushed it open, her smile still wide.

The alarming speed with which her grin faded, and the swift awareness of her scantily clad appearance gripping her would have caused all her siblings to fall upon one another in unrestrained merriment.

Her skin flushed warmer than a late August afternoon spent rowing on the clear, placid waters of the lake at her father's country seat—and, at the same time, a tremor caused her grasp to slip from the latch.

Perhaps she should have knocked.

Or, preferably, remained safely abed.

Before her stood a man, not one of her brothers that she still pictured as boys even though they were two and four years her senior, but instead a true man—stripped to the waist, his back to her.

Thank the heavens above for small miracles.

But to deny that her heart skipped a beat—or ten—would be preposterous. In fact, as Patience stood, unnoticed, studying the man now looking out Merit's open window, she wondered if her heart would ever beat a normal, steady rhythm again or if her skin would ever cool enough to need an overcoat or shawl. It was only when her lungs began to burn that she realized she'd held her breath since opening the door, a call of greeting stuck in her throat.

One utterly forgotten.

So intent on the window, the man failed to notice he was no longer alone.

There was no denying the stranger's presence—an unfamiliar masculine air filled the room. It was both intriguing and frightening. Certainly, she'd witnessed men in various stages of undress, but this goliath was different. Never had Patience been so utterly aware of her own body, while distracted by the sight of another's chiseled form. Her hands itched to reach out at the same time they should be raising to cover her exposed flesh, veiled only by her thin nightshift.

Patience was commonly overcome with indignation, rage, and resentment for those gentlemen who ignored the troubling aspects of society. Emotions she knew well, and how to hide and suppress them. Never had she been attracted to a man, or filled with such…euphoric pleasure at the mere sight of a bare back. Her nipples puckered…if that were even something possible for her womanly buds to do. Her knees trembled, though not with outrage and anger but…titillation.

Voyeurism.

It was what her father had explained drew the large crowds to prized pugilist matches all over the world—and to a certain extent, every *ton* gathering in the country.

Any other day, Patience would have adamantly and vehemently denied that she possessed any amount of voyeuristic impulses. Perhaps she could still claim this to be true if she stepped back over the threshold and silently closed the door, putting an end to the stark, raw nature of the sight before her.

The raw, stark emotion coursing *through* her.

The sensible thing would be to return to her room and never speak of this moment. Deny that it ever occurred.

That was the rational thing to do, and Patience always prided herself on her intellect, even though many in the *ton* considered a female with a mind something to be avoided at all costs.

The man raised his arms high above his head and stretched until he nearly touched the thick wooden beams overhead. He must be at least a foot taller than Patience and stand a head above both her brothers. Damnation, but the width of his shoulders seemed wider than she was tall. Heat pooled at the apex of her thighs as the muscles along his back tensed before relaxing when he put his hands on the windowsill and leaned slightly out to look down the two stories to the garden below.

She knew the view he took in well, though the cover of night with its cloud-covered January moon would mask the thicket of overgrown rosebushes below. It was the same scene she beheld when she gazed out her window in the bedchamber bordering this one. The roses were the only things daring to grow in such a wayward manner. The lawn was perfectly manicured and awaiting a garden party that would never take place. The small hedge maze, truly just five intersecting pathways at the back of their property, was only as high as it was to block the sight of the mews beyond. One side of the lawn, farthest from the stables, was lined with neatly pruned fruit trees that were dormant this time of year, while the other side had been converted to a long-unused sparring area for either fencing or boxing.

Shaking her head, she cast aside all her thoughts about voyeurism and the sights to be beheld outside her window.

There was a man—a stranger—half naked, in her brother's room.

"Sir"—Patience swallowed as the man turned to face her and the heat that had overtaken her face and neck—"please announce yourself and the reason for your presence in my home."

Patience immediately regretted calling the man's attention as his eyes narrowed on her and she took in his battered face: split lip caked with dried blood, knot on his forehead, and the bridge of his nose slightly rounded, betraying the swelling that would be present come morning.

Thankfully, none of the injuries had blemished his chest, or at least, Patience could not see any bruises through the light dusting of hair that covered his flesh. However, she did note the muscles that had rippled across his back and shoulders were also present on his front. In that moment, she'd almost convinced herself that she was scrutinizing nothing more than a prized horse or a champion hunting dog—not the alluring form of a fierce, red-blooded man.

He stared at her, his lips pressed into a grim frown. For the first time, Patience fretted that the man was in her home with dastardly devious and threatening intent. He did not appear a common thief, the likenesses of which were prominently displayed in the *Post* nearly every day. Nor was he outfitted as most burglars would be, with a shirt or tunic or something to cover his tanned chest and board shoulders, and likely something covering at least a portion of his face. He also did not take an aggressive stance or look about with frantic, piercing glances for a weapon or path of escape.

If anything, when his eyes latched on to her, his confidence filled her with an unbelievable sense of rightness.

Yet, it was not right for a stranger to be in her home at such a late hour clothed as he was, nor was it acceptable for Patience to be frozen before him wearing nothing but her nightgown.

Absolutely nothing about her current situation should feel fitting.

It was only when his eyes went from narrowed and assessing to wide-eyed before he turned and averted his stare that Patience regretted her less than suitable attire. Her night shift, while warm, was still white, and she had no corset or other modern device to hide the evidence of her perking nipples through the fine fabric. Could he see that she hadn't so much as donned a pair of the knickers that were becoming so popular in society?

Heavens, her face flamed with heat once more. This was *her* home, and she need give no explanation for her nightly attire.

"S—s—s—ir." Patience loathed the way her voice broke and stuttered over the single word. Taking a deep breath, she began once more. "I asked that you announce your name and purpose in my home."

While she spoke the words without stumbling, they did not hold the warning she'd hoped. They came out as a plea, not the demand she'd intended.

He refused to glance back in her direction, and Patience took the opportunity to take in her brother's room; everything was in its place except for the shirt tossed over a chair near the bed. Red stained the otherwise pristine white linen.

Were his injuries graver than first noted?

"Are you hurt?" She despised the empathy in her tone.

"I was preparing to leave." The deep lilt to his voice sent another wave of pleasure through her as his eyes finally met hers.

"You cannot leave in such a condition," she chastised. How many stories had her mother shared with her about the destitute in Seven Dials perishing due to the cold weather? "You will surely freeze before arriving at your intended destination—although, the frigid temperature will most likely slow the swelling in your nose."

Why in heavens was she giving advice, all but offering to tend the man's wounds, when he was an interloper in her home? He'd still not given his name or his reason for being in Merit's chambers in the middle of the night—not to mention his careless action of opening the window and allowing the coveted warmth to escape into the cold outside.

Oddly still, while he didn't appear scared that he'd been discovered, he *was* nervous and uneasy. She saw it in the way he took quick, shallow breaths and how he leaned forward, tightening his grip on the windowsill, turning his knuckles white.

Patience wasn't as frightened as she should be, though, again, common sense told her that she would be wise to flee the room and seek out the butler—or sound the alarm to wake her father. However, something held her in place and kept her mouth shut as she watched him. Pushing his hair back from his face, he leaned back in and turned to face her.

His hair, sun-kissed—that peculiar color between brown and blond—was long and hanging free like that of a man better suited for the high seas as opposed to civilized London society. On any other man, it would have appeared unkempt, and Patience would have recommended a cut; however, on *this* man, it would be a sin to do away with his long, shiny locks. Hair such as his certainly guaranteed envious looks from every female who passed.

The stranger moved with such swiftness that Patience hadn't a moment to speak before he snatched his soiled, blood-stained shirt and crawled out the window.

She'd been ever so taken by the broadness of his shoulders, the glossiness of his hair, and the expanse of muscle across his bare chest and back that she'd allowed him to escape.

Escape? That wasn't the correct word at all.

Patience hurried across the room and tilted forward out the window. He'd likely misjudged the distance to the ground and was now lying stuck, or worse, injured in the overgrown rosebushes. However, there was no one below. Placing her hands firmly on the window ledge, Patience stood on tiptoes and leaned farther out, looking from side to side down the wall of their townhouse. She spotted the man where he balanced himself on a small strip of wood above the parlor window below. As she stared, he leapt over the tangled, thorny bushes and landed in a crouch on the lawn before looking around and taking off in a sprint toward the drive that led to the front of Marsh Manor.

Not once did he glance over his shoulder—or up at her above.

There was no reason that should hurt her, but it did.

Who was the man, and what had he been doing in Merit's bedchamber in the middle of the night?

Just as quickly as she'd found him, he disappeared.

Footsteps echoed in the corridor, and Patience swung away from the window in time to see her father and their family physician, Dr. Durpentine, enter the room. The tall, thin man wore round glasses that were forever slipping down his nose as he worked. Patience knew the doctor better than most of the *ton* she was acquainted with as he'd been the sole physician who cared for her mother during her final years as the headaches increased and the memory loss and confusion set in.

"Lady Patience," the physician greeted, his sleep-tousled hair the only indication that he'd been deep in slumber before being summoned to Marsh Manor. "I did not expect to see you on this trip."

"Good da—evening, doctor." Patience crossed her arms over her chest, suddenly feeling exposed. "Father."

Her father turned sharply toward her. "Sweet pea? What in heavens are you doing awake at this time of night?"

Could it be that he hadn't noticed her when he entered the room behind the physician? She was well aware of his distracted nature over the last several years—truly, since they'd lost her mother—however, this was extreme, even for him. Perhaps Patience should speak with Dr. Durpentine about the situation.

"I heard a noise, and it startled me awake," Patience explained. "I thought mayhap Merit and Valor had returned home earlier than expected. Who was that man, Father?"

She tried to keep her words unbothered and light, as if the man didn't actually interest her beyond knowing who was responsible for disturbing her rest. Her father knew better than to believe her disinterest as his mouth pressed into a firm line and he silently debated whether or not to give her any information. She'd seen the look all her life. When her mother began to worsen, he'd anguished over how much to tell his children. Each time she asked him how it had gone distributing her pamphlets, he wrestled with how to answer. When she'd asked why no gentlemen ever asked her to dance during her final Season, he'd silently deliberated how to respond. Patience was always saddened to be the cause of his constant inner turmoil, yet she couldn't help but love him all the most for his fierce protectiveness.

Finally, he sighed. "On my way back from Delforte's Hell"—he never shied away from naming the establishments he visited with her pamphlets—"I happened upon a scuffle in an alley. The man...what happened to him, by the way?"

"He leapt out the window." Patience gestured toward the open bank of windows at her back. "Crawled down the side of the house and fled."

"Oh, interesting." The earl shook his head. "Well, I happened upon him and another man, a true n'er-do-well, in an alley. It appeared the thief had set upon him, and I stepped in to assist. Brought him here so Dr. Durpentine could see to his injuries."

The physician chuckled, pushing his glasses higher on the bridge of his nose. "It appears I am no longer needed."

Her father clapped the man on his back with a laugh. "Appears not. I'm confident he'll find a way back to the Albany. We can't help those who do not want our help, now can we?"

"We cannot, my lord."

"Please close the window and run along back to bed, sweet pea." Without waiting for her reply, he turned and ushered the doctor from the room. "May I offer you a drink for your troubles?"

Patience stared at her father's retreating back as he and the physician crossed the threshold and their footsteps retreated to the stairs.

Nothing about her father's detached attitude shocked or concerned her—it was his way of things. However, bringing a stranger—a man, no less—into their home in the middle of the night was very concerning.

Belatedly, she realized she'd forgotten to ask her father for the man's name.

CHAPTER 2

SINCLAIR—SIN—CHAMBERS, the sixth Earl of St. Seville, pushed through the door of the Albany without waiting for the footman and took the three steps down to the walk below as he stared up at the clouded sky above. Bloody hell but his head ached. His lip and nose had swollen during the early hours of the morning, as well. He should have stayed abed for a few more hours. Yet, lying about nursing his cuts and bruises was not a luxury he could afford. At least not if his wounds were little more than a busted lip and a crooked nose. His injuries notwithstanding, Sin had an appointment with Coventry at nine o'clock sharp—and he was much looking forward to speaking with the rascal, especially after last night.

Set upon by a thief. Sin scoffed.

He had no time or funds to play games, nor did his purpose in London include being set upon in a dark alleyway. He'd asked Lord Coventry to arrange a boxing match for him, not have him accosted by a ruffian after Sin had enjoyed several drinks at a local tavern that sold pints of ale for a fraction of the price at the Albany or any of the establishments in Mayfair.

Damnation.

He glanced down the street, mostly deserted at this time of day, and sighed. The breath leaving his mouth stung his lip, and Sin tentatively flicked his tongue along the split to make certain fresh blood hadn't sprung forth. Thankfully, the cut hadn't opened again.

The bloody thug from the night before had gone so far as to steal Sin's coat before fleeing the alley. As if he had the funds to purchase another. Sin only hoped he remembered the directions to the Wicked Earls' Club correctly or he'd be wandering the street. It wasn't as if Coventry and his lot had a sign posted outside declaring the club's name, and London was a new and foreign city to Sin, vast compared to Brownsea Island.

A hackney pulled to a stop before Sin. "Where to, m'lord?"

He thought hard, visualizing the letter from Coventry he'd received at his estate on Brownsea Island. What had the address been? "Bedford Place."

"I know where ya mean." The driver nodded. "I be take'n many fine gents ta 276 Bedford Place."

Yes, 276 Bedford Place.

Sin still had trouble believing that the establishment existed. A club solely for earls. No stuffy, pompous dukes or newly wealthy barons to contend with. Not that Brownsea Island had any of those. It was only Sin, his mother, younger sister, and their people who inhabited the small land mass off Dorset. If it weren't for his current situation, Sin would have gladly remained on the isle, removed from society, content to till the land with his people and take care of his estate.

Unbeknownst to Sin, his father had made that impossible.

The man who'd fled London after his marriage to live out his days in peace and solitude with his family had drained the estate coffers, allowing the land to fall fallow and neglecting those who depended on him. His father had been a private man, a lord who spoke rarely of his estate and their financial stability. Though Sin had witnessed his father corresponding regularly, by post, with his man of business. He'd said it was about this shipping venture or that manufacturing endeavor, but Sin had occupied himself around the estate, not tending the books. By the time Sin had inherited everything, dire straits had already settled on the island folk—and the St. Seville estate.

His only comfort was knowing that even his mother, Sin's constant companion, hadn't known the grim precipice the St. Seville estate was positioned upon.

"Ye be need'n a hack or no?" the driver prodded when Sin remained quiet.

"How far is it from here?" Sin replied, thinking about his ever-dwindling coin. "Can I walk?"

"I wouldn't be advise'n that, m'lord." He glanced down at Sin's new Hessians, his meaning clear. "If'n ye don't find any trouble, it's near a forty-minute stroll ta Piccadilly."

Sin relented and climbed aboard the hack, the chilly morning breeze burrowing straight through his old coat. He still couldn't believe the bloody man had stolen his new coat. Sin's outrage ignited anew.

Thankfully, the driver hadn't mentioned Sin's battered face and swollen nose.

Sin leaned his head back and closed his eyes, trying to ignore the pounding in his temples, as the hack pulled away from the Albany. The least Coventry could do when Sin arrived on Bedford was offer him a drink—or two—to combat the aches in his head and shoulders.

He could not believe the situation he'd found himself in the previous night. Climbing out a window, clawing his way down the side of a townhouse, and fleeing into the night. It was the actions of a rakehell departing his ladylove's abode to avoid being caught by her husband. Perhaps he would have enjoyed the moment more if that had been the case—not that he'd ever found himself enamored with a woman who was already spoken for.

With his golden-brown hair, dark skin, and muscular body, Sin never had any trouble attracting the notice of unattached women.

Images of the ethereal beauty from Desmond's house floated through his mind. Long hair of the darkest brown had hung down her back, her eyes were a cloudy blue that Sin would argue was gray in color, and her skin…its olive complexion had confused him slightly, rendering him unable to speak. Her skin was not dark from the sun as Sin's was. No, it was as if the tone had been inherited. Yet, Sin knew it hadn't come from Desmond's lineage as the elder man was as pasty as a newborn babe—or a prim English rose.

What shocked him most was that he'd been more frightened of her than she was of him. In fact, as her hard stare had traveled the length of his body, Sin hadn't detected even the slightest hint of apprehension. Imagine happening upon a stranger in your home and, instead of sounding the alarm, demanding to know their business.

Sin chuckled quietly, his chest aching from the punches to his rib he'd sustained during the scuffle in the alley. The woman's beauty, poise, and pensive bent had piqued his interest, but he couldn't risk remaining at Desmond's home a moment longer. Not even to verify what he thought was true—the lady was Desmond's daughter. There was too much on the line for Sin to have a man such as the earl asking questions—or worse, summoning the Night Watch to lodge a formal complaint of the attack.

It was best not to occupy his thoughts with the woman or her father; his time and energy were better spent elsewhere.

Sin was in London for one thing, and one thing

only.

To save his family and his people from ruin. It was more than financial ruin, though. It was far more imperative that he succeed at his mission than gain mere money. His people would starve if he did not. His mother and sister would be left without a proper home. There would be no funds to tend the land. His people would have to move away from their properties and find work on the mainland. Families would be broken up, lineages spread across England, and it would all be Sin's fault. If it were in his power to restore security to everyone who called Brownsea Island home, then he would risk everything for that cause.

His father had let everyone who depended on the earldom down, and it was Sin's responsibility to prove his worth to his people. His mother had begged him not to leave Brownsea, his sister had cried as he rode away, and all the while, Sin told himself he needed to fix what his father broke.

It was a solitary mission only *he* could achieve.

And to do that, Sin had to put his trust in Coventry to secure him an introduction into the group of men who organized the grand, bare-knuckle boxing matches that were set for large sums of money. He was a skilled pugilist and took great pleasure in besting all the men on Brownsea Island. Now, it was the simplest means of gaining the large sum of money he needed to keep his people fed and the land around his estate bearing crops.

The hack creaked and groaned as it stopped before a bleak, non-descript building made of sandstone. "This is it?"

"Yes, m'lord," the driver confirmed. "Will ye be need'n a hack home?"

Sin dug into the pocket of his trousers for the few meager coins he'd brought with him. "Ah, no. No, thank you, mate."

For Sin's troubles the previous night, Coventry

would be responsible for seeing him back to the Albany—and perhaps giving Sin a meal to go with the scotch he desperately needed.

He flipped two shillings to the driver and hopped down to the walk to stare up at the building.

The gathering place for the Wicked Earls' Club—formally, The Earls' Guild.

His father had often spoken of the place: a sanctuary where men could find a proper meal, a card game, a fencing match, or far more illicit pastimes.

Not that his father had been the type of man prone to debauchery, even in his youth. Spending all the family coin, yes, that he'd done. Enjoying nights of unsavory entertainments, no. It seemed that unwise and impractical business ventures were Sin's father's crutch. It was only years later that Sin realized it allowed his father to remain hopeful despite the crushing failures that continued to plague his every investment. Had his father and the Earl of Desmond met within these very walls? Had they shared meals together or played billiards?

With those questions came the realization of how truly alone Sin was in London. Besides his correspondence and meeting with Coventry, he knew no one. And in turn, that made him an unknown to anyone in London. Thankfully, Coventry had insisted that he knew a gentleman who would back Sin and help him acquire a few boxing matches, putting up the funds necessary to participate.

The door to the club opened, and a servant offered Sin a welcoming smile.

"The Earl of St. Seville, I presume?" the servant inquired, his speech not that of a common servant but cultured, bordering on educated. When Sin nodded, the man continued, "This way, please. Lord Coventry is awaiting your arrival."

Sin stepped into the building and immediately

regretted not tying his long hair back from his face—or having it cut in a proper fashion. He also lamented wearing his tattered, well-used coat—not that he had any other option. The luxurious interior of the club was unlike anything Sin had ever seen. The sheer amount of wood was enough to keep several servants busy for days polishing, and the floors glistened beneath his boots.

He was lucky he hadn't been turned away and denied entrance.

But then he remembered the reason he was without his finely tailored new coat and the twenty pounds tucked in its inner pocket. His temper simmered, and Sin suspected it would be a task to keep it under control until his meeting with the earl concluded.

He needs must remember, despite what had occurred in the alley, Coventry was his only ally in London—at least until he was introduced to someone who could fix him up with matches worth large purse money. Then…*then* Coventry could go to the devil with his backhanded surprise and take his fancy *club* with him. Sin was an earl, but these were not the men he was used to associating with.

Sin followed the servant through the main room toward a long, narrow hall, staring at the many men reclining in overstuffed armchairs in groups or sitting before the open hearth, reading the London *Post*, conducting business, or simply enjoying a meal.

As he passed a room with the double doors thrown wide, he noted two men embroiled in a gravely serious billiards match. He had the urge to stop and watch—perhaps even join them. To be a man unburdened by the responsibilities of family and his title was something Sin hadn't experienced in many, many years. To be a gentleman with genuine friendships, men—and even women—whom he could speak to of his many hardships and ask for advice, knowing the words spoken came from a place of kinship, was something Sin might never encounter. Taking on the burden meant that others were free of the weight that threatened to crush him. And for that sole reason, Sin would endeavor to keep those he loved disencumbered.

"Lord Coventry's office is down this hall," the footman said, gesturing away from the club's common areas. "If you will follow me."

Sin turned away from the two men and did as instructed.

He was shown to an office, though it nearly mirrored his father's study from Brownsea Island. Books lined every wall, and the earl's desk was neat and organized.

The lord did not stand when Sin entered the room, simply gave a vague nod of welcome as the man's green eyes fixed on him. Was he taking in Sin's size? Perhaps regretting his decision to have Sin set upon by the ruffian? Coventry seemed more than a bit startled by the man before him, and Sin couldn't help but grin. The earl was not what Sin had expected either. The man was at least a decade older than Sin had presumed with his hair already turning a salt-and-pepper grey. His advanced age and greying hair seemed not to diminish his boyish appearance, though, and Sin understood why the man surrounded himself with young earls.

"Have a seat." Coventry gestured to the chair across from him, and Sin noticed for the first time that the coat that had been stolen the night before was laid precisely over the back. "We have much to discuss, and I am a busy man."

Sin responded by collecting his jacket and sitting. He must remember that he was here for a purpose. If he allowed his temper to flare, it could very well ruin any chance he had of winning the prize money he so desperately needed.

That Coventry knew how desperate Sin was only

added to his disadvantage.

He was at the earl's mercy.

Sin knew it. Coventry knew it. And he only hoped that all of London didn't know the extent of his family's financial situation.

When Sin laid the coat across his lap, something shiny and gold caught his eye in the folds of his lapel.

"Welcome," Coventry said as Sin fumbled with his coat to get a better look at what was attached to the newly tailored material.

The bloody garment had cost him more than a year's worth of seed for the field behind his stables. The land would have grown enough wheat to keep his entire estate fed with fresh bread for over six months.

"What is this?" Sin unclasped the gold *W* that'd been secured to his coat lapel as he attempted to keep his shock hidden. The pin itself was no doubt made of pure gold and worth five times more than the bloody coat. "And what do you mean, 'welcome?'"

Coventry reclined in his seat, and his smile widened. "Welcome to the Wicked Earls' Club."

Sin barked a sharp laugh and immediately regretted it when his lip pulled, the wound likely reopening. "I did not come to London to join some club full of arrogant rakehells, Coventry." And why would the earl be foolish enough to think that Sin would trust him after the previous night?

"Come now, my lord…or can we do away with formalities? St. Seville, is it not?"

"Sin, I am called Sin," he grunted.

Coventry slapped his open palm against his desk and chuckled, obviously not noticing the tension lacing Sin's neck and shoulders. "See, my good man, with a name like Sin, you are everything the Wicked Earls' Club was established for."

"I am not in London to meander about town carousing, drinking, and playing billiards, my lord." Had the man deceived him with his letter offering his help? Had Sin been lured to London for ulterior motives? "I will remain in town only long enough to secure the funds needed for my family and my people. If you cannot help me, I will bid you ado and find someone who can."

When Coventry remained silent, Sin pushed from his seat.

The earl held up his hand to halt Sin from leaving. "Sit down, Sin," he hissed. "As I said, we have much to discuss, and from what your letter said, your estate on Brownsea doesn't have much time."

Sin crossed his arms over his chest, his coat clenched in his fist. The fabric would likely wrinkle, but he knew enough about garment care to press them out—that was if a servant at the Albany would allow him use of a press.

"Why did you contact me, and how did you know about my estate's financial troubles?" Sin asked the question that had remained unanswered since he'd received Coventry's letter weeks prior. "My family—and title—is not well-known. We, along with all the St. Seville people, live a quiet, peaceable life on the isle."

Coventry studied Sin intently until the hairs on the back of his neck prickled, and the earl once again gestured for Sin to sit.

When he did, the earl finally broke the silence that had shrouded the room. "Your father and I were once friends. I owe him a great debt."

"And as a way of repayment, you lured me to London to have me accosted and beaten in a dark alley?" The accusation flew from Sin before he could stop himself. He hadn't been certain until he saw his jacket slung across the back of the chair that Coventry had been the culprit. The earl already held an advantage over him there was little need to give him more information to hold over Sin's head. "You—or this club—are not my purpose here…and likely the reason my father chose to leave town before my birth."

"I am uncertain what you think the Wicked Earls' Club is or what we do, but I can assure you, it is not your father's group any longer." Coventry steepled his fingers, and his brow furrowed in thought before he continued. "My men, every earl that belongs to this club, have been hand-chosen and found worthy of membership. Certainly, there are several lords who bask in the more illicit activities available to their station; however, I am dedicated to seeing that every earl under my watch is safe, and his family and estate cared for. Unfortunately, with money and title, these men are easily led astray and give in to their debauched urges." The earl's stare hardened on Sin. "That is not every lord, though. We have men who are much like you: responsible, dependable, and lacking in a certain, what shall I call it, arrogant nature."

It didn't escape Sin's notice that Coventry had yet to answer his most pressing question. Even if his father had once been friends with Coventry, that did not explain how the earl came to know of his estate's troubles. Nor did it mean that Sin should trust Coventry. His father was a good man, but his blindness to the evils of others had ultimately led to Sin's financial troubles now.

"The Wicked Earls' Club is a band of brothers. They help one another. Where one man is weak, another is strong."

"And what of last night?" Sin countered. "Were you *helping* me?"

For the first time, Sin wondered if Desmond had been in on the scheme. He was an earl, after all. Had he been part of The Earls' Guild with Sin's father and Coventry? It made sense…yet made no sense at all. Desmond had been shocked to find him and hadn't known who Sin was until he'd been told.

"I was testing you." It was said with little inflection as if it were commonplace, and Sin should have expected nothing less. "You see—"

"And Desmond, was he part of everything?"

"Desmond?" Coventry betrayed his first sign of unease. He'd been told something he hadn't known. "James Lane?"

"Yes, that Desmond. At least he said his name was James." Sin scoffed. "He happened into the alley and scared off your man."

"Desmond—and his ilk—are from the old generation." Coventry rubbed his jaw. "You—and the men you passed on your way in—are the new. Desmond is a good man, but his eccentric bluestocking of a daughter preaches respectability, duty, honor, and such…which is all fine and good, and very admirable in my mind, but that is not always attainable with the young lot I oversee. One day, I hope all the lords of my club strive to think of duty and honor before their own needs. What did you tell Desmond?"

Sin didn't approve of the way Coventry had described Desmond's daughter; however, he hadn't been long in her company to form his own opinion of her—on anything besides her beauty. "Nothing."

"Are you certain?"

"What was I to say?" Sin sat forward and stared Coventry directly in the eyes. "*Good eve, Lord Desmond. Thank you for the hand, mate. I am in London with the assistance of the Earl of Coventry to secure several pugilist matches with large purse prizes to save my title and estate from ruin. You wouldn't happen to know of any boxing matches in the near future, would you?*" Sin snorted. "I did as any man attempting to keep his true situation from becoming idle gossip around London would do, I accepted Desmond's help and fled out a window of his townhouse in nothing but my breeches and Hessians when he went to fetch a physician."

"Very clever of you." Coventry collected a stack of files from his desk and opened one, scanning whatever was inside.

Sin could not believe the man's lack of concern. "I could have been gravely injured in the alley, or set upon by real thieves after your man left. What if I'd lost my way after departing Desmond's? I could have been taken down by the cold night before finding my way back to the Albany."

Coventry's incredulous stare returned to Sin. "Well, let us be grateful that a few hours out in the elements of London did not bring you to your death because I was able to secure a meeting for you. Tonight."

Sin wasn't certain what he'd expected the earl to say, but that was not it. A sense of betrayal coursed through him when relief set in at the mention of a meeting. "This evening? Where?"

"You will attend a soirée with me. Nothing too grand, just a small ball with a few dozen guests."

"I am to go looking like this?" Sin gestured to his swollen nose and split lip. "I am likely to draw much attention.

"It will be quick," Coventry said. "We will arrive, you will have your meeting, and we shall depart. You may not even need enter the ballroom; however, if you pass on this gathering, I can assure you, you have indeed wasted your time coming all the way to London."

Sin had no other option but to acquiesce. "Where are we to meet, and at what time?"

The smile that overtook the earl's thin face spoke of the man's uncertainty at what Sin's decision would be. He was relieved that Sin had chosen the course he'd set for him.

"Ten o'clock. And we meet here." Coventry closed the file he held and set it aside before standing, signaling that their meeting had come to an end. "I will see you this evening. Do not forget to wear your *W* pin on your lapel. I called in several favors to get this meeting, and the man is under the impression that you are a member of the Wicked Earls' Club."

"Am I not?" Sin inquired, his brow rising in question.

"If that is your desire."

"Very well," Sin said with a stiff bow that brought a new wave of pain to his injured ribs. "Until this evening, I bid you good day, Lord Coventry."

Sin turned and departed the room, keeping his head down until he'd stepped through the front door of the club and out into the brisk morning air, Coventry's final words still ringing in his head: *If that is your desire.*

Desire?

Sin desired to save his family from ruin. Sin desired to fulfill his mission in London and return home. Sin desired to bring safety and security back to his people on Brownsea Island.

Beyond that, Sin hadn't given his own needs much thought.

If aligning himself with Coventry and the Wicked Earls' Club could keep him on course, then, bloody hell, Sin was prepared to accept his place as a wicked earl.

CHAPTER 3

PATIENCE MOVED AROUND the fringes of the crowded ballroom. She didn't flit as her elder sisters did when they traversed about a soirée; no, her movements were more a purposeful stride as Patience studied the people gathered in Lord Holstrom's grand estate. She'd made a list for this evening, and it did not include dancing, flirtatious conversations, or sampling the host's much-revered sherry.

True, this was a social gathering, but Patience had given up on being considered social and proper many years ago. After her first disastrous Season, her father and siblings had held out hope that she would settle in to *ton* life and find a suitable match; however, at the height of her third Season, eligible men of the *ton* had all but run the other way when they saw her coming.

As well they should.

That was precisely how she knew she'd set her sights on the right man.

They had something to hide, and to do that, they avoided conversing with her.

Her father had noted the previous week that Patience would do well to study the difference between conversing and lecturing. To that, she had scoffed and suggested that her father *converse* with his two sons who'd once again been mentioned in the scandal sheets. That had ended her father's lecture quickly enough.

Patience glanced about the room, keeping her faint smile in place, noting that Holstrom was still speaking with several men near the ballroom doors, his back to Patience. Not far from him, his wife, Lady Holstrom, stood alone. Patience hurried along the dance floor and cut behind the refreshment table to stand before the matronly woman.

"Good evening, Lady Holstrom," she greeted. "Thank you for the invitation."

The lady's shoulders tensed in panic when she recognized Patience.

"Ah, well, Lady Patience, I wouldn't think to exclude the Desmond family from such an affair." Lady Holstrom did her best to appear relaxed and stiffly took a sip from her glass. "Where are your sisters and their dear husbands?"

Patience knew full well that she hadn't been invited to the Holstrom ball. She had attended with her sister, Verity, and her husband, who had retired to the card room as soon as their one dance concluded—as social niceties dictated. A little thing like the lack of an invitation was not enough to stop Patience from seeking an audience with Lord Holstrom. The man was rumored to organize pugilist matches all over London— and for heavy prizes, as well. As yet, Patience hadn't received a response from her many letters to Holstrom, but at some point this evening, he'd be unable to avoid speaking with her.

If anyone deserved a *conversation* on the damage sustained from years of bare-knuckle boxing, it was Lord Holstrom.

"Why are you not dancing, Lady Patience?" Lady Holstrom inquired, though the lady knew full well why

Patience never danced. When she lifted her fan, and a small titter escaped, there was no hiding that the woman's question was meant to embarrass Patience. Perhaps her father should speak with Lady Holstrom regarding proper etiquette. "My dear husband and I made certain all of London's most eligible lords were in attendance this evening."

Thankfully, Patience was accustomed to the ways of societal matrons, especially those who had daughters close to Patience's age, and she directed the conversation in a path more suitable to her goals at the ball. "I am certain your daughters, Lady Sarah and Lady Elizabeth, will make sure no lord goes without a dance partner. Although, I do have a matter of great import to discuss with you." Patience fumbled with her reticule and removed her latest pamphlet. If Holstrom were to keep avoiding her, Patience would give his wife the information and beg her to pass it along. "Please, have a look—"

"Oh, Lady Patience, I am sorry to abandon you so quickly, but I think my daughter is in need of me." Lady Holstrom gave her a regretful smile and ignored Patience's outstretched hand that held the pamphlet. "It was lovely chatting with you. Please, give my best to your father."

The matron strolled away toward her daughter across the ballroom, her hips swaying from side to side in time with her extravagant headpiece, not leaving a second for Patience to respond.

Not far from Lady Holstrom, Patience spotted her father as he watched her with a narrowed stare before she rushed to shove the pamphlet back into her handbag. She'd promised her father and Verity that she would not bring her materials to the ball. Deep down, they both had to know it was a lie.

A lie for the greater good, Patience reassured herself. Besides, her father would forgive her. He always did. And Verity…well, Verity had accomplished all she'd wanted in life already: wedded to a duke with several estates. Patience, on the other hand, hadn't achieved anything.

With a forced smile, she nodded to her father and turned back toward the ballroom door as Holstrom disentangled himself from the group he'd been chatting with and slipped out into the corridor.

Brilliant. This was Patience's chance—and likely the only one she'd get during the ball. She glanced over her shoulder to make certain her father no longer watched her; blessedly, he'd moved toward the terrace, his back to Patience.

Tugging the string on her reticule closed, Patience grasped her skirts and hurried after Lord Holstrom. Luckily, the *ton* had become very accustomed to ignoring her presence, so it was unlikely anyone would remember her mad dash out of the ballroom.

She only needed a few moments with him to say her piece. If he didn't listen, then at least she'd have the reassurance Holstrom had been informed of the dangers facing every man who fought in the matches he arranged.

Her mother's fate—her family's fate—did not have to befall another, not when Patience could stop the brutality of the sport. Her stomach turned, her mind traveling to those long-ago days when her mother had fought the sickness dragging her down. What none of them had known at the time was that there was no cure for what ailed Ivory Bess. There was no tonic or salve that could bring back her memories. No doctor who could bring back sensation in her limbs.

Patience was at Lord Holstrom's for a purpose. Swallowing a sob, she pushed on.

She looked left then right after exiting the crowded ballroom and spotted her target sauntering down the dimly lit hall to her right. With the dancing begun and the card room open, no one loitered in the hallway outside the ballroom, which helped Patience greatly.

"Lord Holstrom," she called, her voice echoing down the hall. "A word, if you please."

The man had the same reaction as his wife; however, he halted and turned to face her.

"Lady Patience," he greeted but did not move back down the hall toward her. "Lovely of you and your father to join us this evening."

She'd followed him into an abandoned hall during the middle of a ball, yet Holstrom wasn't the least bit surprised. Inconvenienced, yes. Irritated, most certainly. But shocked to see her trailing him…no.

Patience started toward Holstrom. "My lord, if I may have but a few moments of your time—"

"Lady Patience, do not take me for a fool," Holstrom snapped, pressing the palm of his hand to his forehead as if he'd developed a headache. "I know why you are here and have watched you accost my guests all evening. Lady Holstrom was just speaking of you last week when your latest letter arrived. She fears that if you do not reform your hellion ways, your chances of wedding will soon dry up. I must say, I wholeheartedly agree with her, and I feel it is my duty as a gentleman to speak with your father regarding my concerns."

Speak to her father? Did the man think to frighten her away?

"Not even your father, an earl, will be able to repair your tattered reputation if you continue thusly." Holstrom stared at her, merriment in his smirk as Patience's face flushed.

"You not only misjudge me, my lord, but my father, as well," Patience retorted. "I have my father's blessing to pursue my interests, and there are many things far more important than marriage and starting a family."

"For a woman?" His incredulous tone sparked

Patience's temper. "I cannot think of one."

Patience straightened her shoulders and lifted her chin a notch. "I am saving lives, my lord. At least, that is what I am attempting to do if you would only listen. No one need see the same fate as my mother: memory loss, confusion, swings in demeanor, and loss of feeling in her arms and legs. Families should not have to witness such a fate for those they care for."

It was sorrow that brought the horrible nature of her mother's struggle to her tongue. The disease had not been pretty, and she would never tone down the harsh realities pugilists faced if they continued on their chosen path when relaying her message.

Holstrom could not question the ailments that had plagued Patience's mother, once known as Ivory Bess to all of England, during her final years. Her symptoms had begun long before her father had convinced her to retire from society. As a notorious female pugilist, the Countess of Desmond had lived through many hard years growing up in Seven Dials—even her marriage to an earl could not erase her less-than-acceptable birth.

However, her beauty had won her a few hearts in London.

"Nonsense." Holstrom flicked his arm to the side, a mock way of casting aside Patience's warning. "I have received all the drivel you continue to send round to my townhouse. I have read every word, and it is nonsense, scribbled by a silly chit who should focus her time and energy on her own future as opposed to pestering upstanding lords about their male pastimes."

"Silly chit? I am no such thing, I assure you, my lord." Her voice was stilted, mirroring her frustration. "What happened to my mother could very well hap—"

"Enough, Lady Patience," Holstrom barked, slashing his hand through the air to silence her as he glanced over his shoulder. "I have a meeting to attend to, and I cannot have you carrying on with these outlandish ramblings. Now, be a good little girl and go find your father."

The crackle of the floorboards echoing down the dim hall made Patience's skin crawl. Lord Holstrom wasn't listening to her and would likely never take her concerns seriously.

"Lord Holstrom, I presume?" The voice thundered from behind Patience. "While I am fairly new to London, I do not believe that is any way to speak to a lady. On her behalf, I take great offense."

Patience kept her stare trained on Holstrom, refusing to give up and avert her eyes; however, she listened intently as the man who'd rebuffed Holstrom walked up behind her.

"The Earl of St. Seville?" The man must have nodded confirmation because Holstrom continued. "I was not expecting you for another hour. If you will follow me, we shall conduct our business in my study."

Patience was not acquainted with St. Seville, but if he were meeting with Lord Holstrom it would be wise to properly introduce herself. From his greeting, Patience could have very well found an ally in her cause.

"After you apologize to this lady, I will see her back to the ballroom and only then will we discuss business," the earl said, his tone returned to an acceptable level.

Patience turned to face her white knight. "That is not necess—"

But the words died on her lips.

"It—is—you." Her embarrassment returned as she stuttered over every word. Patience took a deep breath, attempting to slow her erratic heartbeat at the sight of the brawny man who'd only the night before leapt from a window in her townhouse. It was he, yet he was different. His hair was tied back with a length of cord, dried blood no longer clung to his split lip, and the swelling about his face was not as bad as she'd feared. Perhaps the cold of the night had done him some good.

The biggest change, what made her nearly not recognize him, was that he wore a white linen shirt, a cravat, and a jacket. She had to admit, she was a bit disappointed that he was not stripped bare to the waist. "What are *you* doing here?"

"I could ask you the same question," he said. "I think it is very acceptable—and expected—that both of us attend a ball hosted by Lord Holstrom."

Damnation. The man had a point.

He glanced over Patience's head, which wasn't difficult as she wasn't even as tall as his shoulder, and glared at Holstrom. "I am certain you did not mean to insult Lady Patience, Holstrom, is that correct?"

How long had the man been listening to her conversation with Lord Holstrom? A fresh wave of panic and humiliation had her chest tightening at the same time her stomach churned. She didn't know how those two sensations could happen simultaneously, but having a stranger listen to the sordid details of her past was too much to think on.

She continued to stare up at the Earl of St. Seville—she now knew his name—as Holstrom cleared his throat.

"My sincerest apologies, Lady Patience," Holstrom muttered, sounding anything but apologetic. "St. Seville, I will see you in my study once you've returned the lady to the soirée."

Neither Patience nor St. Seville paid Holstrom any mind as his retreating footfalls sounded.

Her neck ached from being tilted back at such a severe angle, though the other alternative was to stare directly at the man's chest.

"The Earl of St. Seville?" she breathed, not sure why it came out as a question.

"Yes, Sinclair Chambers, at your service." Neither looked away. "And you are Lord Desmond's daughter, Lady Patience Lane."

There was no question in his words.

Patience couldn't stop her smile, remembering him clothed in nothing but his breeches while she stood frozen in her nightgown. Taking a step back, her slipper caught on the back of her long skirts.

His hand was at her elbow in a flash, steadying her once more.

Callused fingers clasped her bare upper arms, sending more unfamiliar sensations through her—was it need, desire, yearning?

"Thank you, my lord." Suddenly, Patience needed space. Distance between her and St. Seville. Room between her and the clashing emotions coursing through her. Her anger at Holstrom had dissipated the moment the earl touched her. "I think I should return to the ballroom."

"I will accompany you." His stare searched hers in the dim hallway.

Did he experience the same unexpected emotion at their touch? Certainly not. He was a lord, an earl, a man not unlike those she'd encountered in society. Worldly men who did not hesitate a moment at physical contact.

"That is not nece—" Patience's protest was for naught as the man held out his arm, and she laid her gloved hand at the crook of his elbow. Everything about the man caused her common sense to flee. "Er, thank you."

He swept his hand at his shoulder, likely a nervous habit for a man with such long hair.

When they approached the ballroom, music streaming through the open doors, Patience's pulse settled, and she hoped her cheeks did not remain flushed.

The music and conversation from the crowded room invaded Patience's senses, and for a moment, she longed to return to the quiet hallway—and their moment of privacy. It was a ludicrous longing. The earl was here to meet with Holstrom, and that alone should have warned Patience away from the man. And that didn't even bring into consideration their curious meeting the night before.

Despite all of it, Patience could not deny the need that'd coursed through her—as unfamiliar and unexpected as it was—when the Earl of St. Seville had merely touched her arm. Security, protection, and…salvation. Every emotion wrapped up in that one touch. A desire she hadn't known she'd lacked all these years.

CHAPTER 4

EVERY EYE IN the room settled on them as Sin and Lady Patience stepped over the threshold and into the Holstrom ballroom. It was the exact scene he'd hoped to avoid—that Coventry said he *could* avoid. Arrive, meet with Holstrom, and depart.

Simple.

He could handle his business in London and keep news of his estate's empty coffers quiet until the funds were replaced. His mother had warned him of society's love of gossip, and the imposing sight of him, a stranger, on the arm of Lady Patience Lane would certainly raise some eyebrows and many questions.

Unfortunately, at over six feet tall with shoulders as broad as most doors, Sin was noticed wherever he went. Add to that his busted lip, swollen nose, and long hair, and he was surprised the *ton* hadn't gasped in terror at the sight of him.

What wasn't simple—or foreseen—was coming across Holstrom verbally attacking a woman in the hallway of his home. Sin had immediately acquired a distaste for the lord, and that was before he'd discovered that Lady Patience was the object of the man's scorn. If anyone spoke to his mother or sister in such a disgraceful manner, Sin would be hard-pressed to see the perpetrator properly admonished.

And Sin planned to do just that…but he must remember that Holstrom was vital to Sin's plans in London.

"My lord." Lady Patience spoke quietly to keep anyone from overhearing them. "Thank you for your gallant assistance with Lord Holstrom. I am in your debt."

Her words were lost to him as he took in the peculiar color of her eyes. The night before, he would have told anyone they were gray, but in the glow from the wall sconces, they appeared blue. A lovely, pale shade that contrasted starkly with her rich, dark hair. And her deep blue gown with its high waist, pearl-beaded bodice, and puffed sleeves—this he knew from countless hours listening to his younger sister drone on and on about London fashion—complemented her dark looks superbly.

How in the bloody hell was anyone looking at him with Lady Patience at his side?

"I suppose, as was true of our first meeting, our acquaintance is fairly odd in nature."

Sin focused on her lips, hoping to better understand what came out of her mouth, but his error in judgment was immediate as the urge to draw her close filled him.

"My apologies for my odd behavior last night, Lady Patience. I fear you took me by surprise when you appeared in my room." Why was he offering her an explanation? He wasn't certain, but he kept speaking. "Although we did not have a proper introduction, I feel it only appropriate to have one now. I am the Earl of St. Seville, Sinclair."

"My brother's room."

"Pardon?"

"I happened upon you in my brother's room…in my home." Her eyes widened in mock alarm. "It should have been I who was startled, my lord. As an unarmed lady, that is."

"And yet, despite your lack of weapon, you were not." That had been far more surprising than turning from the open window to find a woman—clad in only a long, white nightgown—standing behind him.

He was making an arse of himself, and all of the *ton* was bearing witness. Sin kept his gaze trained on Lady Patience, fearing if he looked up, he'd find Coventry or, worse yet, Desmond watching them.

"I fretted all night that something dire had happened to you," she sighed. "You could have been injured during your climb down the wall."

"I can care for myself, my lady."

"The night was dark and frigid," she continued. "And there are thieves who set upon unwitting men and women."

Sin wanted to chuckle, but the concern that laced her voice, and the disquieting fact that Sin had, indeed, been accosted before meeting Lady Patience, stilled him.

"I arrived at my accommodations safely enough." The room buzzed around them as the guests returned to their dancing, talking, and drinking, Sin and Lady Patience forgotten for the moment. "And as of this moment, fears of falling ill due to the cold are unfounded."

Silence stretched between them.

Lady Patience wrung her hands where she clasped them before her and averted her stare.

"How much did you hear?" she whispered in a rush. "It was meant to be a private conversation between Lord Holstrom and myself."

"Only Holstrom's ungentlemanly retort," Sin lied. There was something in the way she wouldn't meet his stare when she asked how long he'd been listening that stopped him from confessing the truth. Hearing her speak of her mother's illness had been a violation of her privacy, and in a way, Sin could understand. "However, I could not remain unannounced after hearing his vile words."

His answer seemed to satisfy her because she nodded slightly, and her hands dropped to her sides.

There was no doubt that Sin would feel the same if someone overheard his private conversation with Coventry or learned of his estate's peril.

"I must go." Sin heard the regret in his tone and hoped that Lady Patience didn't recognize it, too. "I do not wish to anger Holstrom further by my tardiness; however, I intend to chastise him once more for his deplorable manners."

"That is not necessary, my lord." She finally brought her stare back to his, and Sin wanted nothing more than to forget about Holstrom, Coventry, and the looming ruination of his estate. "I am quite used to such behavior where Holstrom and his kind are concerned."

Was this what Lord Coventry had been speaking of earlier that day? His words sprang to mind: *"bluestocking of a daughter."* If Sin were asked, he'd describe Lady Patience as enchanting, passionate, and precocious.

Thankfully, no one asked Sin for his opinion.

"Before you go"—Lady Patience loosened the drawstring on her handbag and retrieved a folded note—"take this, please. Give it to Lord Holstrom. Certainly, he will listen to you." She glanced past him, and her shoulders tensed. "It is past time I return to my father. Thank you again, my lord."

He was left to watch her walk away, clutching the folded sheet of paper in his hand. He should be content that his meeting with Holstrom was no longer delayed...but he would not dwell on why he was overwhelmed with discontent as the distance between him and Lady Patience grew.

FOR THE SECOND time in one day, Sin found himself in an unfamiliar room, seated before a man he was unacquainted with. How many years had he lived on Brownsea Island—his entire twenty-eight summers—never meeting anyone new? Fifteen, twenty?

The room was sparse, furnished only with the necessities a man might need when working or sharing a drink with a comrade. Sin knew well enough he was no friend of Holstrom's, which suited him perfectly. Besides the massive, finely constructed desk that resided between them—almost a way of showing Sin how superior Holstrom was to him—there were several chairs, a sideboard heavy with decanters, two shelves lined with ledgers, and a large, unlit hearth. The lack of a fire and the cold that hung in the room was likely another ploy Holstrom used to his advantage. Sin, little more than hired help, was not worthy of his host wasting money on heating the room.

Consequentially, there was little motivation for Sin to impress Lord Holstrom. The man had been reserved and quiet since Sin took the seat across from him. He wasn't sorry for the way he'd spoken to Lady Patience; however, he at least had the good sense to be ashamed of what Sin had witnessed. It was a start for a man as powerful and wealthy as Holstrom. The day would come when Sin would be in a better position, and showing Lord Holstrom the error of his ways would not put Sin at a disadvantage. Until that day, he had to play by the man's rules.

Sin needed Holstrom more than he needed Coventry.

That hadn't seemed possible mere hours before.

"St. Seville, please take a seat," Holstrom began, setting aside the letter he'd been reading when Sin entered the room. If he'd known he would be made to wait, Sin would have halted outside Holstrom's study to retrieve the folded paper Lady Patience had given him. Instead, it remained in his jacket pocket for future perusal. He had no intention of handing it over to Holstrom or anyone else. "Lord Coventry has written me about your prowess with fists. However, I am inclined to take his writings of you with a grain of salt due to your"—he nodded at Sin's split lip— "appearance."

"Call me Sin," he said, ignoring the man's implication.

Holstrom's eyes brightened at Sin's childhood nickname. It was not as many thought. *Sin* had nothing to do with him committing any transgressions or any lack of moral character, it was simply easier for his younger sister, Juliette, to pronounce when she was a babe. Unfortunately, or fortunately in this case, the name had stuck. Many read greater meaning into the name, mainly because of Sin's sheer size and privateer appearance. The dusting of hair on his cheeks and chin, in combination with his long locks, was enough to make most people think he was a swashbuckler and a tyrant of the sea.

"Sin." Holstrom tapped his chin. "Sin. I think it suits, especially if you are the skilled pugilist I've been told."

"I am." There was no need to say anything further; the man could take Sin at his word or send him away.

"Why have our paths not crossed until now? I am acquainted with every pugilist worth their salt in all of England—and many from France and beyond."

"This is my first time on the mainland, besides going into Dorset for provisions." Sin despised appearing the uncultured man he actually was; however, there was no other explanation to give. His family had lived away from society since his birth. "My estate is on

Brownsea Island."

Holstrom sat forward in his chair. "How can you call yourself a prizefighter if your skill hasn't been tested against that of other elite boxers?"

"I *call* myself nothing, my lord," Sin retorted, reclining in his seat as if Holstrom's opinion mattered not a whit. "I am an accomplished pugilist. You can arrange a match to gauge my proficiency, but I do not fight for free."

Lord Holstrom laughed at that. "Unproven with an arrogance paralleling that of the great Gentleman Jackson. I cannot say my curiosity is not piqued; however, paying your way into a match and putting my coin on the line is much to ask without any proof that you can actually win."

"Set up a match with a small purse prize," Sin said with a shrug.

"What skilled pugilist would agree to a match worth virtually nothing?"

"I would suggest you advertise the fight as one that my opponent is certain to win." Sin reclined farther, resting his entwined fingers at the nape of his neck and tilting his head back to gaze at the ceiling. "Or find another unknown fighter. Either way, I will be victorious, and then you will secure matches for the large prizes I have heard about from Lord Coventry."

Holstrom scrutinized him across the expansive desk, and Sin understood why men of his status chose to meet in such rooms, with large distances separating them: Holstrom relished the power and control it gave him. Sin wasn't as certain about Coventry. Sin never met with his steward or stable master with anything between them. They stood or sat as equals during all their meetings.

"Will Lady Patience be an obstacle to your success?" Lord Holstrom inquired.

"Of course not."

"That is not what I witnessed in the hallway," he countered.

"I would have spoken as I did if you'd been speaking with any member of the fairer sex, my lord." Sin straightened in his seat as Holstrom scowled. "I also thought it in our best interest to not garner additional notice by Lady Patience if she did not suspect our *involvement*, though I would be foolish to think our association has escaped her notice after our meeting in the hall."

"Discretion is key, especially where Desmond and his daughter are concerned." Holstrom's scowl faded as Sin's actions became clear, or at least what Sin wanted the man to believe. "It is not wise to spark Lady Patience's temper or suspicion, with her history and such."

Besides the prizefights, this was the only topic of conversation that drew Sin's interest.

Everyone seemed to speak around Lady Patience, instead of directly about her.

Temper, eccentric, bluestocking…

It was nothing Sin had experienced with the lady. She was peculiar, but in a way that kept his attention. Wise but not arrogant. Beautiful but not vain. Forthright but not offensive. Why was it only Sin who noted those qualities?

"You have convinced me, St. Seville." Holstrom riffled through papers to his left until he found what he sought. "Yes, here it is. There is a match, two days hence—"

"What is the prize amount?"

"Does that matter?" Holstrom growled. "You wanted an opportunity to show your skill. I am giving it to you."

"As I said before, I do not fight for free," Sin retorted, glaring across the desk until Holstrom sighed in resignation. "What is the prize purse?"

"Ten thousand." He set the paper aside and smiled. "A small prize, by some standards, but enough for now. Win, and the coin will double, or possibly triple for your next match."

It was more than Sin had expected to win for his first fight, but he couldn't let on, or Holstrom would certainly take advantage of him. Instead, Sin sat forward and appeared to ponder the offer before nodding in acceptance.

"Excellent." Holstrom chuckled. "I think our partnership will benefit us both. The buy-in for the fight is two thousand—"

"Buy-in?" Sin asked. Coventry hadn't spoken of any such thing.

"The fighters put in money with the hope of seeing it returned, sometimes tenfold." The man seemed unconcern with Sin's surprise. "I will put up your money for this first fight. After that, I will secure matches, and pay your way in, unless you prefer to put up your own money. You will learn the way of things soon enough."

Lord Holstrom stood, signaling that their meeting was over—much as Coventry had done.

Behind Sin, the door opened, and a footman waited to escort him out.

"I think it best you do not remain for the soirée." He cleared his throat and gestured toward the door. "My dear wife does not take kindly to mixing business with pleasure."

Sin hadn't planned to attend, only find Coventry and leave; however, the man's curt dismissal had Sin disliking the lord even more. He needed to remember that Holstrom was his only connection thus far. In time, he would not be beholden to the rascal, but until that day came, he needed to play nice and follow Holstrom's rules.

His estate's future hung in the balance.

CHAPTER 5

PATIENCE LEANED FORWARD, pulling the drapes aside to peer out the carriage window once again. The cold evening air pushed into the interior and sent a shiver through her as she watched the building. Gentlemen—and servants—came and went at an alarming rate, yet the one she sought still had not presented himself. As the time passed, Patience worried that the Earl of St. Seville would never leave his accommodations at the Albany.

Night would fall upon London within the hour, and Patience needs must return to Marsh Manor or risk her father finding out about her unchaperoned excursion. Eventually, he would discover her trip to the Albany, but Patience had always been the type to act first and ask for forgiveness later. Much as she'd had to do when her father had confronted her about bringing the pamphlets to the Holstrom soirée.

This would be yet another occurrence her father would be angry about, but he would certainly pardon her within a few days.

This was her second evening stationed outside the Albany while her father took his nightly meal at his club.

"We should be heading back, my lady," her driver called from his perch.

"Not yet," Patience hissed into the growing dusk. "Ten more minutes, please."

She was uncertain if she'd see St. Seville coming or going at all. Perhaps he'd moved accommodations or departed London altogether.

The urge to thank him once more for his chivalry hadn't left her since he escorted her back to the ballroom two nights prior. She'd gone so far as to remain close to the doors in hopes of speaking with him after his meeting with Holstrom but he hadn't returned to the soirée, and Patience had been relegated to spending hours hidden in her carriage outside his lodgings.

It would be a lie to say that she was only here to thank him again.

Damnation. She wanted to know if he'd given the pamphlet to Holstrom, and if he'd read it.

She knew there were rumors swirling about an upcoming prizefight with a purse of ten thousand shillings. It was a fortune for many pugilists, such as her mother who'd grown up without much to her name. For Ivory Bess when she was Patience's age, it would have been the difference between being able to rent a room in a decent lodging house and having food for a year or being homeless and starving. She winced at the reminder of her mother's difficult past. She'd suffered hardships Patience and her siblings would never truly understand.

Men would continue to fight if lords with deep pockets, those such as Holstrom, organized and funded the matches.

She gained a bit of hope when St. Seville had championed her before Holstrom. Especially after years of being ignored and labeled a nagging, bothersome, disagreeable, and willful hoyden. But St. Seville apparently saw her in a different light. She could tell by the way he actually listened to her and didn't cast off her words as nonsense. Because of this, Patience had a renewed sense of purpose. She'd even spent the entire day creating a new cautionary piece about pugilism. With any luck, she would have it printed in the *London Daily Gazette*. How could they deny her? The *Gazette* happily posted weekly columns that did nothing but bring ruination upon members of the *ton*. Certainly, they would not refuse to circulate information that could *save* lives as opposed to ruining them.

The nightly lamplighter sauntered by her carriage, carrying his long rod and pack, continuing down the walk in preparation of his evening duties. It was the same as the previous evening, and Patience knew that, soon, the night watchman would amble past on his way to the alehouse down the road.

Predictable.

Much in life was predictable, never changing—like the lamplighter and the watchman.

Patience sighed, propping her elbow on the window ledge and catching sight of another man leaving the Albany—too short, too round with hair that could only be described as thinning.

Her sisters had entered society, made successful matches, and were starting families. Her brothers were embroiled in what society called the age of sowing their wild oats before they eventually settled on proper wives and started their own families.

Predictable.

What no one had predicted was the hardship and loss Patience would suffer—along with her father—when her mother's ailments finally brought her life to an abrupt end. Five years later, and it was as if it had happened only yesterday. One day, her mother, while sometimes forgetful and prone to clumsiness, was there; and the next…she was gone.

"That is him, my lady!" Her driver thumped on the top of the carriage, pulling Patience from her melancholy. "Over there."

Patience leaned out the window but could not see where the driver was pointing.

Just as she feared, all her time had been wasted, and she'd missed his departure from the Albany. But Patience spied St. Seville when he paused to greet the lamplighter.

"My lord!" she called, but only succeeded in garnering the notice of five other gentlemen within hearing distance. She bit her lip, unsure what to do. She'd promised her driver that she would remain in the carriage at all times, but if the earl disappeared down the block or waved down a hackney, Patience would lose sight of him quickly. "St. Seville!"

The lord turned sharply and searched the street as if he weren't certain that someone had actually called him.

Patience waved again, and his eyes landed on her, his brow pulling low as he lifted his collar and strode toward her carriage.

"Lady Patience," he said as she leaned back into the window and pushed the door open. "Whatever are you doing here?"

He halted several feet from the door and surveyed the interior of the coach.

"Are you alone?"

"Do get in, my lord, before someone notices me," Patience cautioned. Instead of entering the carriage, he looked up to where her driver was perched. "I am letting all the warm air out."

Patience sat back with a huff and tapped her boot on the floor. Why was he being difficult?

Finally, he stepped up into the carriage and took the seat across from her—and she marveled at him once more. The interior of the carriage shrank with his bulky frame taking up the entire seat across from her. Normally, the bench fit both of her brothers or Patience and her two sisters…comfortably.

St. Seville's massive width left no room for anyone else on his side.

Coincidently, due to the close quarters, she could see that his lip was healing nicely and would likely not leave so much as a tiny scar when fully mended.

A flutter in her stomach, the type she felt when she rode in a carriage going a bit too fast or while riding a horse that was slightly untamed, had her shoulders tightening with tension. Anticipation or apprehension? It was like in the hallway outside Holstrom's study but magnified a thousand times. He was so close she felt his heat.

If she dared, would she be so bold as to reach forward and run her gloved fingers along his healing lip? Perhaps remove her glove to place her bare fingertips against the stumble on his jaw? Would the hairs be coarse like that of a horse's mane, or soft and glossy like Patience's own tresses?

"Lady Patience, please tell me your father does not approve of you loitering outside a gentlemen's lodging house." His gruff tone rankled her. "This is highly improper and could jeopardize both our reputations."

Another man thinking every woman lived only to preserve her character. Had she misjudged him? There was much more to life than living as dictated—an unlimited number of experiences women of the *ton* went without due to propensity and decorum. There was freedom to be obtained when a woman cast aside all that was expected of her and embraced her passions. Her mother had stayed true to her heart, and Patience would endeavor to do the same. But how, exactly, was Patience to explain that to St. Seville?

"I came to thank you once more."

"That is not necessary," St. Seville said with a firm

shake of his head. "It is what any gentleman would do in those circumstances."

No man, besides her father, had ever spoken up in her defense. St. Seville could argue the point, but he'd never lived in Patience's place, and he did not know the mean-spirited nature of London gentlemen.

"Be that as it may, I am very grateful, my lord." Patience hadn't come to argue over some trivial notion of what counted as gentlemanly conduct.

"How did you know to find me here?" he asked, his voice softening, though he still sat stiffly across from her, his shoulders tense.

"I overhead my father speaking with the physician the other night," she said with a shrug, attempting to hide her embarrassment over the fact that she'd listened as intently as she had to any morsel of information about him. Since that night, her father hadn't so much as mentioned St. Seville.

Crossing his arms, the earl reclined slightly. "Is that all you needed to say?"

Patience's stare drifted to the drape blocking her view of the business London street beyond. Did she dare voice what she'd truly come to ask? Would he think she'd used him for her own benefit? None of that mattered overly. Patience longed to know if Lord Holstrom had considered her pamphlet at all. What St. Seville thought of her was irrelevant and would do nothing to champion her cause.

It would be wise for her to keep that in the forefront of her mind; spending her time wondering what this gentleman thought of her was a waste.

"You want to know if I gave Holstrom the paper." It was as if he'd read her mind.

Her eyes snapped back to his, but she tried to cover her interest in the topic. "I had wondered." Patience would not betray her eagerness to know what had happened to the paper for it would cast a bright light on her own needs.

"Holstrom made it very clear how he felt about you and your meddling"—He held up his hand when she opened her mouth to protest—"his words, not mine. I think we both know I do not share the same views as Lord Holstrom. However, I regret to inform you that I did not pass the paperon to him. He would have tossed it in the rubbish bin as quickly as he took hold of it."

Patience deflated, her confidence seeping from her. "I commend your honesty, my lord."

"However," he continued, giving Patience pause. "I read the pamphlet. *The Trials and Hardships of Caring for Aging Pugilists.*"

He quoted the pamphlet's title perfectly. There was no hiding her utter shock as her eyes widened, and her pulse raced.

"I found the information very informative and thought-provoking."

Patience slumped back into her seat. "Unfortunately, the men that most need the pamphlet and knowledge refuse to listen."

It was her luck that someone had actually taken her work seriously, only to be someone not in jeopardy.

"Why do you spend your time trying to help those who do not want your assistance?" he asked.

He didn't mean it as an offense, Patience could tell. St. Seville was genuinely interested in her reasoning. Could it be that there was someone among the *ton* who was unfamiliar with her lineage and past?

"My mother—the once notorious Ivory Bess— died from the injuries I write about in my pamphlets," Patience whispered, lowering her stare to her gloved hands, clenched tightly in her lap. She couldn't bring herself to meet his stare, for fear he'd be like so many others. Many in the *ton* lacked a certain amount of empathy. "The physician treated her for years. It started with almost imperceptible things like forgetfulness and being overly clumsy, but progressed quickly to complete loss of large pieces of memory and an inability to use her arms and legs."

He seemed to listen and truly think about each word she said, which pushed her to continue. It had been years since she'd spoken so candidly about her mother to anyone besides her father. The many times she'd lamented to others had been met with scorn or outright dismissal.

But not St. Seville.

"She passed not long after my fifteenth birthday." Patience breathed in deeply to stop the sob that threatened to escape. She would not cry in front of the earl. She could not bear losing the tight grip on her control. There was only one thing left to say on the matter, and then she could tell him farewell and allow the tears to come when she was alone. "The doctor believes, as do my family and I, that her ailment was caused by her years as a pugilist before she wed my father."

It was hard to believe her mother's fate had been sealed long before she met her husband, wed, and started a family. Ivory Bess was destined to die before any of her children reached the age of majority. It wounded Patience deeply that so many others would see the same fate if they did nothing to protect themselves against it.

His hand landed on hers, squeezing gently, and she brought her gaze back to him.

Patience wiped at her cheeks, mortified by the dampness she brushed away. "I have not spoken of this to anyone but my family."

He leaned forward until only mere inches separated them, his interest in her—in her past—so intense it pulled them closer in the confined space.

"I am so sorry you lost your mother," he breathed, and sorrow permeated the interior of the carriage. "I cannot imagine how difficult it was for you and your family. That burden is a heavy one to bear."

For some odd reason, Patience suspected he knew exactly what it was like following the death of a loved one, especially one as close as a mother. She wanted to inquire about the depth of his loss but did not dare. They were little more than strangers. True, she had seen him in a most indecent manner in Merit's bedchamber, and he'd stood up for her when no one else would. When he'd grasped her elbow to stop her from falling at Holstrom's ball, it was as if his touch were as familiar as that of any loved one. And then, he'd comforted her only a few moments before as if they'd sat just so and discussed the hardships of life on a thousand different occasions.

Perhaps Patience *was* the silly girl Lord Holstrom accused her of being.

She blinked several times to keep additional tears from pooling in her eyes. "Again, my lord, you are too kind."

The warmth from his continued touch could be felt through her glove, and even though it was foolish to admit such, it was welcomed. Several years ago, those around her had stopped offering the comfort Patience sometimes needed, the reassurance that her feelings—heartbreak, sorrow, and even anger—were justified.

She brushed at her cheek, unsurprised to find another wayward tear had slipped down her face. "My apologies, my lord, it is only that I am very passionate about educating others about my mother's fate. I know it is silly to allow my temper to flare when others don't heed my advice. I am working on that."

Patience let out a light laugh, but it was piercing and hollow even to her own ears.

St. Seville had fallen silent, his hand leaving hers as he pushed back onto his bench. Not often did someone listen to her—truly hear her—without voicing his or her own opinion and objections to her plight. Her siblings routinely reminded her of her peculiarity. Her father reprimanded her for nearly every infraction, yet at the same time, ignored her for days at a time. And that was not even considering the responses from men such as Holstrom. She'd begun to think, though she was loath to admit it, that she was making no difference, her tales of caution falling on deaf ears.

"Nonetheless, I thank you and will not keep you any longer." The words rushed out of her mouth. She was close to falling apart, and she would be damned if she embarrassed herself further in front of the earl. The ache in her chest intensified as it always did when grief was close to overtaking her. "I will not keep you from your evening."

He moved toward the door, and Patience could only imagine his need to depart the carriage and be away from her.

Halting, his hand on the latch, he offered, "I am meeting with someone, and it would be impolite to be late. However, I should see you—"

"Then you should be on your way with all due haste, my lord." Patience knew he was going to offer to see her home, but she could not be the cause of his tardiness.

"I suppose I could…"

"Do not even ponder that idea," Patience said with a hesitant smile. "My driver will take me home safely, just as he brought me here. There is no need to worry over me. Your friend—" She stumbled over the word, for the first time thinking he might be on his way to see a woman. Why did that fill her with dread? And make her stomach harden with…envy? Certainly, Patience should not feel a spike of jealously over a man who was nearly a stranger to her. She'd come to the Albany to thank him, not entangle herself in his life. "Your acquaintance will not be pleased if you are late."

"The Earl of Coventry is not one to be kept waiting," he readily agreed.

The Earl of Coventry. Not a woman, after all.

Patience's relief was short-lived when the street lamp outside was lit, and the new glow glinted off the golden *W* pinned to St. Seville's lapel. The pieces fell into place, and Patience felt foolish that she hadn't suspected the connection before now.

"You have taken up with the Wicked Earls' Club, then?" Her tone was stilted, and any trace of warmth for St. Seville vanished when she dragged her glare away from the golden pin to search his face for deception. "I suppose I should have known."

Her hurt was unmistakable, and Patience made no effort to hide it as she glanced away from him toward the covered window.

"No, Coventry is—er—*was* a friend of my father's," the earl explained, his posture as tense as Patience's. "He offered his assistance and guidance while I'm in town, that is all."

Patience snorted, not bothering to mask her disdain for the group that went by the atrocious name. It was as if they were proud to flaunt their wealth and status, all while shirking their responsibilities and going on in a manner most unfitting an earl.

"I am certain that is all; however, be warned, Coventry and his ilk are a depraved lot," she said, her eyes remaining on the thin fabric covering the carriage window. "They are uncouth and embroiled in all manner of debauchery."

"As I said, Coventry is a family friend. I am in town for the sole purpose of my duty to my estate and family." He paused, and Patience felt his eyes on her, all but begging her to look at him. She would not give him the satisfaction. Again, she reminded herself that caring for this stranger did nothing to advance her cause. "When my business is completed, I will return to my family home, and I have no plans to set foot in London again, nor consort with the likes of Coventry and his *men.*"

"My father was once friends with the Earl of Coventry, too," Patience confessed.

"And your father once knew mine," St. Seville countered.

"He was part of The Earls' Guild?" Her stare snapped back to his. Her father had said nothing of knowing St. Seville's family. "The Guild is all but disbanded now after Coventry came into power. My father loved and cherished the men he saw as more than friends. To him, they were family. When my mother died, my father could have used their support. Instead, Coventry refused him entrance to their club. The new lords of the Wicked Earls' Club could not be bothered to help one of their own. Coventry hasn't changed, I fear."

"Again, I am sorry. And you should know, I haven't any allegiance to the Wicked Earls' Club or any man who calls the place home."

Patience studied his expression: open, sincere, and without any hint of dishonesty.

"Very well, my lord." Patience smoothed her gloved hands down the front of her skirts. "I will not keep you any longer. There is no need to give the Earl of Coventry my regards."

He chuckled and pushed the door wide before glancing outside. He turned back toward her. "I bid you good evening, my lady. As I have listened to your advice, may I be so bold as to offer my own?" When she nodded, he continued, "Meeting with men unchaperoned at dusk could lead to scandal and ruin. Do take more caution with your reputation."

He leapt to the walk, and Patience called after him, "If I were concerned with such things, I would have changed my ways long ago, my lord."

This time, his response was unrestrained laughter, not the reserved chuckle from before. The sound was like the sweetest melody, and she thought in his normal life he must laugh often—it sounded natural. What would it be like to wake to such laughter each morning, or fall sleep with the same melody in her ear at night? It was far different than the silence that had settled upon her home and her family of late.

"Noted, Lady Patience," he called and closed the door before calling to her driver. "Please return your mistress to her home with all due haste."

"Yes, my lord." Her driver pulled the brake, and they were off in the direction of Marsh Manor.

Patience leaned back into the velvet squabs of the coach. How had she been at first pleased to see St. Seville and comfortably entranced with him, only to have her skin prickle with anger at his acquaintance with Coventry? Even now, she was uncertain how she felt about the man or why she wanted nothing more than to explore whatever it was that drew her to him.

Knowing the earl and discovering what secrets he held would not benefit her.

He was best forgotten, or the distraction he caused her might very well throw her off course.

Patience folded her arms across her chest, determined not to ponder where her hands would rather be.

CHAPTER 6

SIN STOOD ON the fringes of the growing crowd at Bedford Square—not to be confused with Bedford Place where Coventry's club stood. A mistake Sin made which made him even tardier than before. The sun had fully set behind the buildings bordering the square by the time Sin had watched Lady Patience set off for home. He'd hailed a hack outside his lodging and made the mistake of venturing all the way to Bedford Place before redirecting his driver.

The vision of Lady Patience steadfastly waiting outside the Albany had distracted Sin, nearly causing him to forget his purpose in London.

Of all the people he was acquainted with in town— not many, as it were—Lady Patience had been the one on his mind. Her bold, tenacious actions would be celebrated in any man, but with a woman it was seen as improper and damaging to her future. It made little logical sense to Sin. Though those exact tendencies were what kept the lady in his thoughts. And now, knowing of her heartbreak and sorrow, there was yet another layer to her complex nature.

Oddly enough, the one virtue she lacked was her

namesake—patience.

She was quick to form an opinion of Sin based solely on his connection to Coventry and his meeting with Holstrom. Yet, that was something he and Lady Patience had in common. How swiftly had Sin recognized that he loathed Holstrom? The man had only spoken a few words, but they were enough for Sin to realize that he was not a man to be trusted. That did not diminish the fact that Sin *needed* Holstrom and his connections in the pugilist realm if he had any chance of bringing his estate back from near ruin.

He felt horribly about Lady Patience losing her mother—and in such an awful manner—but could the physician say for certain it was due to her past as a female prizefighter? His skirmish from the alley told him there was danger in fighting, especially when the purse prizes were more than some men earned in a year of hard labor, but Sin couldn't allow the drawbacks to alter his course.

Sin pulled the collar of his coat higher to block the wind as he securitized the crowd for any sight of Holstrom or the match that was to be fought. His height allowed him to see over the heads of most men and across nearly the width of the square, at least as far as the lamplight stretched. There were a large number of men and some women milling about the open area, far more than Sin had expected for the lateness of the day. Lamps had been lit before his hack arrived, shrouding the area in a hazy glow of yellow made thick by the fog that had rolled in from the water lying nearly stagnant in the Thames.

The din of the crowd—raised voices, laughter, and a few argumentative shouts—washed over Sin. Besides the absence of the bright sun overhead and the fresh coastal ocean breeze, Sin could almost believe he was back on Brownsea Island, working alongside his men in the fields or in the stables. However, he would not risk closing his eyes to immerse himself in the dream. He knew firsthand what could happen on a dark London street if a man let down his guard. Being set upon again was not something Sin could afford.

No, he needed to keep his wits about him, best his opponent, and collect his purse.

Not dream of home or a lady who had no place in his future.

That wasn't exactly right. It wasn't she who had no place in his future, it was who Sin was not of her world. She lived in town, wore dresses of the finest silks and satins, and attended society as expected. She wasn't London's usual demure, polite debutante but neither was she made for the hard life on Brownsea Island. Sin was a man made whole by his work on his lands and caring for his people—not his knowledge and skills when surrounded by the *ton*. Sin felt more at ease in a pugilist ring than in a London ballroom.

The truth was, there was no place for Sin in her world.

Lady Patience would one day belong to someone. And it would not be him.

She would wed, have a family, and remain where she belonged—in London. No matter how much she protested conforming to society, Sin suspected one day, no too far in the future, she would find her place. In society and the world…and both would be better for having her. Brownsea Island may as well be on another continent, for their paths would not find one another again once he left town.

There had been no reason to lie to her about where he was going or whom he was meeting with. He owed her nothing. Yet, after listening to her speak about the tragedy of her mother's death, Sin could not bring himself to tell her that he was going to do the one thing she would beg him not to do. There hadn't been any need to discuss his plans at all.

He'd lied to her. Worse still, she believed that he'd truly been set upon by thieves the night Desmond found him in the alley, not that he'd practically begged for the attack to prove his mettle as a fighter. He was a willing participant in it all. It should not weigh heavily on him that she was perhaps more than a little correct about him.

He *had* fallen in league with the Wicked Earls' Club, albeit reluctantly.

"St. Seville." A hand landed on his shoulder, and Sin swung around, prepared to defend himself if Holstrom, much like Coventry, thought to test his skill. Fortunately for the man—and mayhap unfortunately for Sin's nervousness—it was only Lord Holstrom who stood behind him, his hands raised with palms outstretched. "Didn't mean to startle you, mate."

Sin brushed his cheek, a gesture he'd grown as accustomed to as lacing his boots, but his long hair had been tied tight at the nape of his neck, an inch above his collar in preparation for the coming fight. Both boxers would be shirtless, and Sin made certain his opponent had no opportunity to grasp his long locks. The rules of pugilism were not known for their fair nature.

"Is the match set?" Sin growled.

"Of course," Holstrom scoffed and nodded to two men at his side. "This is Albert Paulson and Gerald Crone.

"Evening, gentlemen," Sin replied, eyeing the pair. One man—Paulson—was too old to be a fighter, and the other man, while dressed like someone of the lower class, lacked any muscle to speak of. Neither was his opponent.

"They represent Gus Povolti." Holstrom spoke slowly as if Sin were too daft to understand. "The man you will be fighting."

"Very well." Sin made a show of glancing around each of the men. "Where is he, and how are we to have a fair match with this crushing crowd?"

The two men laughed, the younger man doubling over at the waist as if Sin had meant his question as a jest. When he didn't join in on their merriment, both men sobered, and Sin turned to Holstrom for an answer.

"The *crush* is here to watch you fight."

"Me?" Sin asked, unable to understand how they knew of the match and why they'd come out at this time of night to see him fight.

"How do you think a match pays the winner ten thousand pounds?" Holstrom countered. "These people have not only come to watch the prizefight, but they have also wagered their own coin on the outcome."

Sin knew his portion to participate—which Holstrom put forth for him—was two thousand. He figured the other fighter matched that amount. As for the remaining six thousand…Sin had misguidedly thought Holstrom was responsible for collecting it. Similar to an investment venture or the like. Why did the thought of so many people watching him fight cause his stomach to churn and his palms to perspire? Most of Brownsea Island had watched Sin box since he was a lad of around nine, and he hadn't lost a match since his fourteenth birthday.

But an entire square of strangers, most with a wager on the line?

He wasn't ignorant to the rules of prizefighting; he'd watched two matches when he first arrived in London while he was waiting to meet with Holstrom. The fight he'd watched the night he was accosted near Covent Garden had been small with only a handful of spectators. The rules were clear, though Sin hadn't expected such an audience. His stomach hardened, and his head swam as he glanced around the square.

"Green, he be look'n green, Holstrom," Crone crowed. "This be simple as pie for ol' Gus."

"We shall see." Holstrom retorted, eyeing Sin. "I think my man here will be the first to best Gus."

A cheer went up in the center of the square and Sin, along with Holstrom, Paulson, and Crone turned as the crowd pushed back, creating an open space to reveal a man. The lad, already bare-chested, stood a head shorter than Sin and had about half the muscle. Gus Povolti bounced from foot to foot and rotated his shoulders back to the crowd's utter delight.

Why had Sin envisioned the match completely differently: a dimly lit warehouse with a handful of spectators, similar to the fight he'd witnessed. Two men coming together with fists raised for a fair fight.

But this—Sin swept his glare across the square—was an utter circus.

He, with his younger sister in tow, had traveled to Dorset once when a traveling show moved through town. There were performers and exotic animals galore. The crowd had cheered and jeered when the lion tamer had nearly lost his hand when the beast decided he did not want to obey the man's commands.

At the moment, Gus Povolti was on display—and he relished every second of it.

Soon enough, Sin would need to strip and take his place, preparing for the fight. All eyes would be on him. Would the gathered people cheer him on or shout for his defeat?

Did it matter? Sin was a winner. He'd always been a winner and now was no different. He'd hedged his entire future on this moment, used most of the funds left at his estate to journey to London with hopes of tripling the coins until he had enough to support his people.

Defeat was not an option.

Leaving London poorer than he arrived was not Sin's plan.

Unsettling dread weighed heavily on his shoulders.

"Are you ready?" Holstrom hissed near his ear.

Images of his homeland—the unhurried movements of his people, the light lapping of waves at the small beach area by his home, and the fresh ocean scents—vividly streaked through his mind. Those were the reasons he was here. To keep worry from his people. To make certain many generations of St. Sevilles reveled in the waves against the shore. And had the opportunity, year after year, to breathe deeply of the intoxicating aroma of his homeland.

Yes, he was ready for the coming match.

When Sin only nodded, keeping his eyes trained on his opponent, Holstrom stepped into the widening circle and threw his arms out. He grinned for the crowd as everyone fell silent.

"Ladies and gentlemen," Holstrom called, spinning in a circle. "Fishwives and merchants. Tavern maids and drunkards."

The square erupted in loud applause as men threw their fists to the darkened sky, and women shouted their pleasure before once again falling quiet.

"You have been promised a prizefight to overshadow all other prizefights, two pugilists who've never before entered a match against one another. Gus 'Lightning' Povolti comes from Prussia and strikes hotter than a lightning bolt." Holstrom raised his arms, giving the crowd ample time to cheer before glancing in Sin's direction. His story was not so grand nor worthy of applause. "And his opponent, directly from the coastal isles of the East, is the Earl of S—" He paused for a moment and smirked as if debating St. Seville's name. "—the Earl of Sin!"

Every stare trained on Sin where Holstrom pointed his out-stretched arm at him. Some gasped, others cheered, but every person nearest him took a large step back as he was waved into the inner circle.

"Yes, my fine London citizens," Holstrom

continued, obviously enjoying his place as commentator. "He is modeled after a Roman god and raised near the sea, his body molded by hard labor and the unrelenting sun."

The Earl of Sin?

He wanted to hide himself from the dramatic nature of the event; allow the crowd their spot of fun but remain withdrawn from the stares and jeers.

Instead, Sin set about unbuttoning his coat and removing his crisp, linen shirt, pulling the fine garment over his head. The action only served to have the crowd breaking out in another round of shouts and cheers as men—and many women—held up purses of coins or stacks of notes.

"What is going on?" Sin leaned close to Paulson, who'd remained close to him.

"Bet'n, milord," Paulson chuckled. "It be no surprise if'n the prize purse be double the ten thousand after they be see'n ye without your shirt. Though they be wise not ta count out me fighter."

Sin stared around the square as Holstrom and another man collected whatever coin or notes the crowd held out and scribbled in a small notebook. Perhaps he would garner the money needed for his estate faster than he planned.

Paulson clapped Sin on the shoulder with a grin. "Don't be count'n out ol' Gus too quickly, hear. He be one'a the best fighters I be see'n since me father took ta the ring."

With that, the man hurried over to Sin's opponent and whispered something in his ear, to which the fighter nodded and glanced in Sin's direction for the first time. Gus showed no signs of being startled by Sin's sheer size. Neither did Sin see the man as a fighter he couldn't best. One solid, accurately placed jab, and the man would fall. If there was one thing Sin was confident in, it was the power of his fists.

"Fighters!" Holstrom pointed to Gus and then to Sin. "Take your places."

At the call, the crowd inched in, leaving Sin no other option but to move to the center of the square to face his opponent, fists raised and ready.

Sin was here for his family. He was here for the future of his estate. He was here to make a better life for everyone on Brownsea Island.

Sin held his clenched fists before his face, stepping from one foot to the other as the other fighter did the same, though his feet moved much quicker.

He would best Gus "Lightning" Povolti. He would prove his mettle.

Confidence surged through Sin, and his shoulders relaxed as he eased into his usual fighter's stance.

And then he would fight again.

CHAPTER 7

PATIENCE PULLED UP to the square, her brow furrowing in confusion to see so many people—men and women of the *ton*: shop owners, dock workers, orange sellers—all gathered tightly at Bedford.

"Stop here," she shouted over the cheering of the crowd, even as her heart thundered in her chest. At first, she hadn't been certain what had made her instruct her driver to double back and follow St. Seville's hack; however, at the sight before her…it was obvious. "I will depart here."

"My lady, I cannot—"

Patience hopped from the carriage and turned her narrowed stare upon her driver. "I shall be well, I promise. How many days did I spend coming to gatherings like this with my mother?"

Allowing her voice to crack would have signaled Patience's torment at the spectacle before her.

It was a prizefight.

Patience had accompanied her mother to enough matches to know what was to come. Ivory Bess may have retired her pugilist pursuits when she wed the Earl of Desmond, but that did not mean her passion for the blood sport had fled with her vows. Instead of fighting, her mother had trained other pugilists, both men and women, in the age-old art.

St. Seville had been on his way to meet Coventry to watch a prizefight, even after everything she'd shared about her mother? He'd been empathetic to the point of reaching out to comfort her with his hand upon hers. She hadn't imagined the impact of her words on him. He'd listened, he'd heard, and Patience had *believed* he cared.

What lay before her negated all of that. Invalidated everything she'd expected of St. Seville.

Her first impression had been correct: he was no different than Lord Holstrom and the men of the Wicked Earls' Club. Perhaps even worse as those men didn't seek to keep their true natures hidden.

"I will wait here for you, my lady," her servant shouted over the raised voices.

The match was preparing to start, and the crowd did as was common, they began chanting as each selected their fighter.

Some shouted "*Lightning*" while others chanted "*Sin, Sin, Sin.*"

Patience had been away from the training clubs frequented by many of the pugilists in London for the last several years after her father had bid her not to return. The anguish that always followed her visits only served to remind her of everything she'd lost. That was why she'd originally set her mark on the men who organized and funded the sport.

Patience's pulse beat ever faster as the cheering grew in intensity. There was a time, in her youth, when attending a prize match was exhilarating. She'd taken on the role of her mother's shadow. She'd watched her train others, and helped her demonstrate various moves and defensive tactics. Up until her mother had grown unable to walk, Patience had reveled in the experience, doing everything asked of her to make her mother proud. For a time, it had been their personal secret that, one day, Patience would enter a match of her own. Her father would have never allowed it, and knowing what she knew now, Patience would rather swim the murky Thames than step into a ring and risk injury. The loss of a dream, even one as foolish as her own career in the pugilist world, had filled her with a great void until she adjusted her path in life.

The crowd suddenly fell silent.

The match had started.

She searched the gathering crowd, two or three people deep, trying to spot St. Seville and Coventry, but her height and proximity prevented her from attaining the optimal view. Gathering her skirts, she dashed back to her waiting coach. Without warning her driver—for he would have surely attempted to halt her—Patience climbed aboard the boot at the back until she could see over the heads of the crowd. There was no reason for Patience to remain at Bedford Square. The Earl of St. Seville and his interests shouldn't concern her. Getting angry or hurt by him, a man she'd only met a few days prior, was preposterous.

Yet, she continued scanning the gathering for the earl. He shouldn't be difficult to spot as he towered over most men, and his shoulders were certainly broader than two average men combined.

"Where are you?" she mumbled.

What she planned to do when she *did* locate him was still a mystery. A tongue-lashing? Perhaps she only needed him to know that she'd seen him at the fight and let him watch her walk away, never to speak to him again. Again, Patience was well aware that her behavior was only justifying the names she was called in polite society. What other option was available to her, though? Her father had been distributing her pamphlets for over a year, and still, no one had heeded her warnings. She was going about things with single-minded determination…with no changes. How much more could she do before she gave up and gave in?

She determinedly kept her stare averted from the men in the center of the square. Nothing good would come from witnessing two men pummeling one another until one fighter drew blood, collapsed, or signaled defeat. Though the sounds, so familiar and once upon a time comforting, did nothing but increase her pulse. Something that should never again excite her had an odd effect on her in the present. Her senses betrayed her, and Patience worked to still her racing heart.

She refused to allow violence to thrill her.

A collective gasp disrupted her search, bringing Patience's attention to the pugilists.

People began to chant once more.

"Sin, Sin, Sin."

One man, bare-chested, staggered back, catching her notice.

She knew the exposed chest, even from this distance. Broad and etched with muscles strung tight. Arms as round as thick tree limbs with breeches tightly covering Herculean legs corded with the same brawn.

The Earl of St. Seville—*Sin*—regained his balance and advanced on his opponent, who countered the move by shuffling in a wide arch away from Sin's long-reaching fists.

The earl may have the muscle and strength to throw a damaging blow, but he lacked the speed and agility of his opponent, who weaved and moved with the skill of a man trained under the likes of John Jackson. He flitted about the ring made by the crowd as if his feet didn't actually touch the ground, while St. Seville lumbered in his wake, far too heavy on his feet.

Had no one taught him the need for balance and the advantage of remaining poised on the balls of his feet?

The small, agile fighter ducked under Sin's outstretched arm, swept forward, and brought his clenched fist up to connect with the right side of Sin's jaw. If she were closer, Patience would have likely heard his neck snap back sharply from the blow.

Sin appeared dazed for a brief moment before shaking his head stiffly and blocking his opponent's next swing.

Brawn and raw strength would only get a prizefighter so far.

If St. Seville didn't move his feet and put some distance between him and his opponent, he was going to be defeated...and quickly.

The skill of a pugilist was threefold, as her mother always said. A good fighter had two of three things: brains, brawn, and speed. A winning fighter knew he had to possess all three.

Sin—the fighter, not the lord Patience had thought she'd come to know—wasn't aware of his weakness. And because of that, he would lose.

She should pray that would not be the outcome, but the surety that filled her with regards to her intuition left no room for doubt. The Earl of St. Seville would need more than her prayers.

"Separate!" The shout came from the far side of the square, and Patience spotted Lord Holstrom. "Fight."

Two things were perfectly clear to Patience in that moment: her father had mistakenly rescued St. Seville from a fight he'd wanted, and Sin had been at Holstrom's ball with the purpose of meeting about this very match.

She'd been foolish to worry St. Seville was off to meet a woman, and had thought that, perhaps, Coventry was worse; however, the true knave was Lord Holstrom. At that precise moment, Patience would have preferred St. Seville to be roaming about, courting a woman or ensconced in Coventry's club.

She'd been stupid to believe that the earl had meant anything he said to her, even chastising Holstrom for his improper behavior toward Patience had been a ruse. Holstrom was a devious man, but the earl was far worse because he was the same as Holstrom. Yet, he took it a step further by lying to her about his intentions. At least Holstrom didn't hide anything.

Had the two men laughed at her foolishness after Sin had returned her to the ballroom?

Heat flushed her body, and her stare hardened on the fighters.

The duplicitous lord deserved a sound thumping.

As if hearing her thoughts, Sin's opponent dipped to the left and brought his right arm around, his fist connecting with Sin's temple, sending sweat flying into the crowd as Sin grunted.

The pugilist known as Lightning raised his fists in victory when Sin dropped to the ground.

Her stomach twisted in a knot tighter than a fighter's fist when she realized that the match was officially over and Sin had, as she'd predicted, lost.

The crowd jeered and moved in tight to congratulate the victor and hurl insults at the defeated boxer. Her heart sank further when she noted that Sin remained on the ground, barely pushing himself into a seated position as Lord Holstrom stalked across Bedford Square.

St. Seville had pledged himself as Holstrom pugilist, and he'd likely had quite a bit wagered on the earl's head. When he lost, Holstrom abandoned him, standing on the far side of the square in conversation with a group of gentlemen. The crowd quickly dissipated as those who'd lost their bets moved on, and those who'd been victorious claimed their winnings and headed off to the local alehouse or, if they were wise, home.

And still, St. Seville sat in the square, his head hung in defeat.

Patience was hard set on him reaping what he sowed.

He'd lied to her. He'd done worse than omitting the truth with the intent to deceive her. Their entire time in her carriage had been meant to distract her from his true intentions. She hadn't asked the correct questions; satisfied with his explanation that he was in London to help his family. Outrage licked at her chest. Something within her demanded that her fury and…hatred for this man and his sport be vocalized. Why would a gentleman in his prime—a lord who knew the repercussions of such an unnecessarily brutal sport—risk his well-being when he had a family waiting for him to return.

Despite her anger and disappointment, Patience couldn't leave him. The blow that had struck him down was obviously hard enough to give Sin an excruciating headache and induce confusion. She'd spent years regretting that no one—anyone—had been there for her mother when she needed help. If someone had taken notice of her mother before her father had, she might have been spared the cruelty of her death.

And Patience and her siblings would have been blessed with many more years with her.

Perhaps the Earl of Desmond would not be the empty shell he was today had his love not been taken from him.

Never could Patience leave another in need, especially when she had the power to save them.

She scrambled to the ground and called for her driver to follow suit.

She and the servant pushed through the milling crowd until they reached St. Seville. His lip had been split wide once more, and his ear bled, a trickle of blood already drying.

"My lord." Patience dropped to her knees at St. Seville's side and grasped his face. His pupils were large, leaving only a thin outline of brown around the edges. "Sin." When had the name come to represent the earl in her mind? "How many fingers am I holding up?"

She drew her hand back far enough for him to focus on it and held up her gloved fingers.

"Two," he muttered.

"Very good." Patience turned to her driver. "Collect his shirt and coat. We will meet you at the carriage when he is able to stand."

"I will carry him."

"No, please, collect his belongings and prepare the carriage to depart." Patience wanted no one, including her servant, to see St. Seville in such a state. Just as her father had been her mother's only caregiver during the worst of her deterioration, it was dignity Patience attempted to give Sin, despite his lies. Glancing around, she noted Lord Holstrom making his way back toward them, his thunderous expression certainly meant to incite fear in those he planned to confront. At that moment, his outright glare was focused on St. Seville. "I think it best we depart. Can you stand, my lord?"

"Of course." He made to push to his feet, and Patience slipped her hand under his arm to assist him. Perhaps she should have accepted her servant's assistance. If the earl had a difficult time remaining on his feet, he could send them both to the ground. "What are you doing here?"

His eyes focused on her before widening and glancing around the square as the crowd continued to disperse. He hadn't realized it was she at his side.

"You should not be here," he muttered, but she heard his voice grow stronger with each word.

"Your lip is busted open again, and your ear is bleeding," she replied sternly. "Let us make it back to the carriage and then we can talk."

When he nodded, they started toward the street. The crowd had dispersed enough that no one blocked their escape.

"St. Seville!" Holstrom shouted, and Patience felt every cord in Sin's back tense. "A word."

They remained facing the street with Holstrom at their back.

"We needn't stop, my lord," Patience prodded.

She wanted to be away from the scene, not that it would erase it from her memory or allow her to forget the jeers of the crowd or the sound of fists hitting flesh. Patience took another step toward her waiting carriage, but Sin pulled from her grasp. His head had cleared enough that his balance had returned. It was always the way of things her father had said. Those harrowing moments after a particularly brutal punch when the fighter couldn't remember where they were, let alone their own name. It faded quickly, and so did the panic and terror of the episode, leaving only an incessant thirst for another match.

The physician had explained that it was akin to the draw of opiate dens for those dependent on the substance.

Patience watched helplessly as Sin strode back to Holstrom, his chin held high despite the almost unnoticeable limp in his step.

They stood twenty paces away, and Patience couldn't hear what was said, but Holstrom spoke, and Sin nodded before he turned and returned to her. It wasn't her right to ask what was said or why Sin had lied to her. "My carriage is up ahead," Patience mumbled, unsure what to say as her fury at his deception clawed at her still. "My driver collected your discarded shirt and coat."

"I do not need your assistance. I must return to Lord Holstrom and speak with him about…" His entire body tensed before he winced and allowed his shoulders to relax once more. "Thank you, Lady Patience; however, you did not—"

"You will return to Marsh Manor, and Dr. Durpentine will be summoned." She did not reach out to assist him again but walked slowly by this side. "Your lip needs tending, and you will perhaps need laudanum for the vicious headache certain to come."

"I can tend to my own wounds, Lady Patience." Walking side by side, Patience felt the heat radiating off his shirtless upper body—was it anger, embarrassment, or resentment? It did not matter, nor did his misguided notion that she would forsake him now when he needed her.

She had to occupy her mind with thoughts of his injuries. The alternative was the anger, hurt, and betrayal already there. Her emotions were illogical and suspect. She knew this, but was still unable to stop them from coursing through her.

"Home," Patience called to her driver when she and St. Seville finally made it to the carriage. The streets around the square, only moments before jammed with people, horses, and carriages, were now clear as the spectators moved along.

"No." St. Seville halted, turning to her. "I can find my own way back to the Albany."

"You are hurt." Bloody hell, Patience shouldn't care that he was injured. It had been his own foolishness that had led them to this point. "It is after dark, and the air is growing chilled with night. But if you prefer to hang on to your pride, I can leave you here in the coming cold. Perhaps you will find your own way home, or…your injuries may be more profound than you realize, and they will hinder you quicker than the elements."

Patience shrugged when Sin glanced at her waiting carriage and her driver. It was his decision—as it had been her mother's all those years ago. She could not force help upon those who did not want it. "Mayhap Holstrom will show mercy on you if there is a bit more blood coming from your lip and nose."

Sin exhaled, and his gaze softened.

"At least allow me to see you back to the Albany," Patience prodded.

Her driver held out Sin's shirt and coat, and the earl quickly slid them on, officially transforming himself from Sin—the *pugilist*—to the Earl of St. Seville. His split lip, quickly bruising eye, and the spot of blood near his ear were the only lingering remnants of the fighter Patience had witnessed for the first time just moments before.

Reluctantly, he acquiesced and followed her into the carriage.

They both took the same seats as earlier in the evening when she'd caught him outside the Albany—on his way to fight. Yet, before her was not the man she'd come face-to-face with in her brother's room a few nights prior. Nor was he the lord who'd championed her against Holstrom at the soiree.

Though neither was he the fighter she'd witnessed at Bedford Square. Her fury dissipated.

Could the Earl of St. Seville—Sin—be all of those things yet none of them at all?

Were there additional complexities to him that Patience had yet to learn?

They both remained silent as the carriage hurried through the dark London streets toward the Albany. Patience had too many questions milling about in her mind, the answers to which may or may not wound her more than watching helplessly as Sin's opponent pummeled him.

Could Patience wait feebly in the crowd as the Earl of St. Seville—or any other fighter—risked his life at this violent sport?

CHAPTER 8

SIN COULDN'T BRING himself to look at Lady Patience during their short ride back to the Albany. There'd been nothing to gain by withholding information from her—nor anything to lose. They owed one another nothing…not even honesty. However, he'd deceived her all the same. His attempt to save her from the hurt and pain that would come if she learned of his destination had failed. Miserably.

Perhaps his mistake had been thinking he could honor his promise to his family and not hurt anyone in the process. Never had his plans included meeting a woman such as Lady Patience. Hearing her heartbreaking tale and then embarking on the exact path that would bring it all back to her.

He longed to apologize. He *should* apologize.

His course in London could not be altered for a woman who would soon be out of his life. He was in town to secure the money needed to save his family.

Sin had every intention of fighting again.

Desperation and shame brought a sheen of sweat to his palms.

It was no longer all about saving his family. Now,

he owed Holstrom, who'd lost a great deal of money when Povolti had struck Sin down. He could not return to Brownsea Island more heavily indebted than when he left. It was unthinkable.

Lady Patience wouldn't understand. She was the daughter of a wealthy earl, not the heir to an impoverished estate with too many dependents to number. If he failed, it would mean that his mother and sister would suffer, and his people would either starve or be forced to find another place to call home. All to appease a woman who would likely never want for anything in her life.

He could sense her stare on him, and again, he had the urge to beg for her forgiveness. It would be an empty outpouring on his part, though. Sin had been a fool to think he alone could save his family. His father, despite his best efforts, hadn't possessed the gumption to lift his destitute estate from the shambles he'd created for them—why did Sin think he could do any better?

"Sin," Patience whispered into the silence that had overtaken them. "Is that what you prefer to be called?"

There was no warmth in her voice, no sense of familiarity, and he knew he deserved any tongue-lashing that might come his way. If nothing else, at least for his betrayal of her most private pain. The loss of her mother had wounded her deeply, and Sin had listened to her anguish, yet it hadn't stopped him from pursuing his course of action. She'd shared a piece of herself with him…and only him. It didn't matter that they were little more than strangers, her confession had bound them together in a way he'd never known with another.

"It is what my family—and my close friends—call me." Suddenly, he desperately wanted her to call him by the name, as well.

"It fits you," she sighed.

His eyes snapped to hers in the dimly lit carriage, and the chill that had overtaken him after the rush from the fight fled. He wanted to demand that she continue. "*How does it fit me*," he longed to ask, but the carriage had halted, and she drew back the material keeping them from view. He should call to the driver and ask him to continue on, take them to Bedford Square and back again in hopes that she'd continue talking. Despite her bluster and bravado, there was much to Patience that Sin had yet to discover. Namely, why he felt the overwhelming need to please her despite their short acquaintance.

"We have arrived, my lord."

Sin should thank her for seeing him to his lodgings and depart. Return to the solitude of his room in the Albany to see to his injuries and ponder how he'd lost his first match.

"You know that brute strength alone is not enough to succeed as a pugilist." She set her narrowed glare on him, the animosity clear in her tone as if his very attempt at boxing offended her. She turned back toward the window before uttering her next words. "You are a fool if you think your sheer stature is enough to secure a spot as a prizefighter."

"I have never been one to think anything comes easily, my lady," he retorted. Except he'd done exactly that coming to London. "Though my brute strength—as you call it—does provide some advantage during my matches."

She chuckled, the sound deep and rich with zero hesitation. "If you say so."

"Are you saying my size and muscles are a disadvantage?"

"No." She paused, and Sin thought she might not continue, but she sighed. "As loath as I am to admit it, I learned much from my mother. Your size gives your opponent a bigger target, making accuracy not as important. Also, your heavy frame decreases your agility."

Working the estate, his raw strength had always been enough. Never had he shirked from the physical demands of his land and people. Even in his youth, Sin could lift the weight of three farm hands. He'd relied on his strength more than he now cared to admit in front of this small, scowling female. "I have spent many years training at my estate. While I was not familiar with London's prizefighting rules, I am not an utter simpleton with regards to pugilism."

She huffed. "Obviously, you did not receive the correct type of training."

The carriage door swung open, and Lady Patience held out her hand, her driver assisting her down to the walk in front of the Albany. Thankfully, the street was nearly abandoned this late, most men already having departed for their evening entertainments and the hour too early for them to be returning home.

He had little choice but to follow her as she marched up to the front door of the Albany and nodded to the footman who opened it. The servant visibly paled at the sight of Lady Patience as she whisked into the building. It could not be uncommon for the fairer sex to visit the lodging house, but one so obviously of the peerages was probably rare.

She paused inside the foyer and glanced over her shoulder at him. "Which way, my lord?"

"Pardon?" he gulped.

"To your room," she said slowly. "Which way?"

When Sin didn't immediately respond, Lady Patience pivoted toward the footman with a wide smile. "Sir, as you can see, the Earl of St. Seville has been injured—possibly suffering from an addled brain—and I must get him to his room."

"Up the main stairs, third door on the left, my lady." He bowed low. "Do pull the bell cord if you or my lord are in need of anything further."

"Very good," Lady Patience inclined her head to

the servant, and Sin watched as the man blushed and hurried off down the hall.

Sin stood in stunned silence as she started for the stairs, her chin held high. Anyone who saw her—and once again, he was thankful that no one but the footman was present to see them enter—would think she owned the Albany.

Pausing, she glanced back at him, and Sin's heart about leapt from his chest.

She intended to venture to his room. Certainly, she did not mean to go so far as to *enter* his private chambers?

"Do you need assistance to master the stairs, my lord?" Her tone was too cordial, especially when one factored in his deceptions. She was almost teasing him. "I can call the servant back if you think it is needed."

Sin cast off the shock and disbelief of Lady Patience entering his lodging house and trailed her up the stairs, doing his best to keep his eyes from her hips and bottom, which were at eye level. Perhaps Povolti had managed to rattle his mind with his hits, after all. A headache was, as Patience had stated, not long from setting upon him.

They walked side by side, his hand grazing hers only once as they traversed the wide hall and halted before his door.

"This is my room." Sin immediately regretted his obvious proclamation. He cleared his throat. "Thank you for assisting me to my lodging."

"Do you have a friend you can call upon?"

"I am new to London, but do not worry." He glanced down at his boots. "This will not be my first occasion tending my own wounds."

"The jarring blow to your head may cause delayed impairments or mask a more serious injury." She leaned up on her tiptoes and stared into his eyes. "Are you dizzy? Is your stomach roiling? Are you overly tired?"

Sin wanted to laugh. No one had made such a fuss over him since he was in knee breeches. "I am not dizzy nor is my stomach unsettled. As far as my exhaustion, I find myself in a rare state of extreme awareness."

He would rather perish than admit that his keen alert nature had naught to do with the prizefight and everything to do with the simple fact that Lady Patience—her deep brown hair swept up into a loose knot—was standing directly outside his bedchamber door.

"Nevertheless," she chastised, her tone severe. "I will remain until I am confident you are well enough for sleep."

"Y—y—you mean to remain here? At my lodging?" Sin stood before his door, barring her entrance, his heart thumping loud enough to echo down the stairs and into the foyer.

Lady Patience—in his room—alone. It was far more intimate than their time in her carriage.

She glanced up and down the hall. "Unless you will agree to accompany me to Marsh Manor, then yes, I will remain at the Albany."

Men would be returning within the next few hours from their evening entertainments and, at that point, there would be no possibility of her slipping from the house unnoticed.

Boots sounded on the stairs, and Sin turned quickly and fumbled with the latch on his door. At least if they were in his room with the door firmly shut, no one would spy her. Sin would deal with getting her safely back to her carriage when he was certain no one would witness her presence.

Once inside—with the door shut—Sin stood with his back to it, afraid to enter the room any farther, despite Lady Patience's ease. She glanced about the room before moving toward the hearth and lightly running her finger along the mantel, pivoting to face the large four-post bed in the far corner. For the first time, Sin flushed with embarrassment. His room at the Albany was nothing more than a large bedroom that also served as his dining room, sitting room, and study. His wardrobe was only a small cubby. Thankfully, the Albany offered servants to act as his valet when needed because Sin's limited funds would not have extended to cover a larger suite of rooms nor lodging for his servant above stairs.

He could not watch her any longer, her slow, deliberate survey of his private space. He'd found lodging at the Albany, but besides his things lingering about the room, this place was not his, nor did it represent him.

Sin moved to his dressing closet and the looking glass that hung a few inches lower than necessary for a man of his height. The fight had split his lip open again as she'd mentioned, and Sin suspected the cut would not heal now without leaving its mark. His left eye had a bit of black budding to the surface, indicating the excellent placement of Povolti's final blow. The prizefighter had surpassed Sin's expectations, and he was not fool enough to deny he'd underestimated his opponent. The fighter had been light on his feet in a way Sin would never be able to replicate. Swiveling his head from side to side, Sin hissed at the pain that shot down his neck and into his back. A thin trail of blood had escaped his ear and dried as it traveled to his neck. He'd fought against many men on Brownsea Island, even journeyed to Dorset to test his skills on the mainland; however, never had he worried about injuries. Or worse, death.

"I do not understand, my lord."

He stared into the mirror, not at himself but at Lady Patience behind him as she dipped a cloth into the bowl on the washstand. She wrung the excess water from the material and stared at him.

Her words were lost to him. The only thing he saw was the elegant curve of her neck, the rosebud shape of her red lips, and the slate grey of her ever-changing eyes as she watched him in turn. Even in the subtle glow of the candles situated about his room, Sin could see the confident glint in her eyes, and the sureness of her steps as she crossed the room to stand before him. She was a woman filled with the resilient nature that came from knowing her worth, her inner strength, and her unwavering belief that if tested, she could care for herself.

Had Sin ever possessed such confidence? Surely, he'd been filled with grandiose ideals and drive when he made the decision to journey to London, but he'd quickly learned the hard way that being in a foreign city, surrounded by strangers, made him far too dependent on the few people he was acquainted with. Something Sin had now come to realize was a grave mistake.

She placed the wet cloth to his lip, lightly pressing to cleanse the cut.

Once more, she captivated him. Not her beauty, for that had never been in question, but her desire to help him even though she'd lived through the horrors of her mother's ailments. Patience had followed him to Bedford Square and had thrown caution to the wind, all while being at his side when he needed her. Sin could have made it back to the Albany on his own, but having Patience hurry to his aid was a measure of comfort he hadn't experienced since leaving Brownsea Island and his family a few weeks prior. He hadn't realized he missed the closeness he and his mother and sister shared.

"I do not understand," she repeated, moving the cloth to the blood near his ear.

"What?" It was the only word he could utter as he once more focused on the sensation of her hands on his skin. When had she discarded her gloves? Sin glanced in the mirror once more to see their white lengths crumpled near the washbowl. "What do you not understand?"

"You said you were in London to help your family."

"I am," he replied without hesitation. "I did not lie about my purpose for being in town."

"Why then would you put yourself—your health and well-being—in jeopardy?" Her stare never left his neck, and her soft, warm touch brushed his shoulder as her hands fell back to her sides. "It would not serve your family well if you were gravely injured."

"It is what I came to London for." Shame coursed through him at the confession. "My estate is destitute; my family and people will continue to suffer if I cannot earn the coin for future crops and repairs to my land and holdings."

"And you think to gain the necessary funds by prizefighting?" The disbelief in her tone was akin to a dagger to his heart—and his pride. Sharper than any punch.

It had been the extent of his plan, and as unorthodox as it was, he longed to share it with her. If only to help her understand. "I was not in possession of enough funds to invest in a business venture to attempt to double or triple my share. I wasn't blessed with an education at one of the elite universities of England, nor have I associated with many men of my class. I lack the means to increase my family's coffers in any way but with my talent in the ring."

Surely, she could understand that. However, he couldn't bear to meet her stare. She would see his embarrassment, his desperation—and his waning hope.

So many people depended on him…and him alone.

"It is something I excelled at on my estate," Sin said with a shrug, attempting to downplay the importance of his words despite their significance for both him and his people. "And I had read news clippings about how men—and women—could earn their weight in pounds and change their entire lives by entering several matches."

"It is not too late to change your course." She moved back to the washbowl, her steps slow and measured. "I am certain my father can help, if it is only money you need."

Sin shook his head, wishing it were that simple. The option of taking a loan, borrowing money from either the bank or another wealthy peer, had been discarded quickly. While his land and people might be destitute, at least they were beholden to no one. Only Sin held the note to his lands and that of his people. If they starved, they would starve together, yet they would still remain in control of their land. No one, not the bank or another, could take that away from them.

And he had no intention of letting his people go hungry.

"Prizefighting is not the only way," she sighed.

"Unfortunately, my choices are even more limited now." Sin remembered Holstrom's parting words before he and Lady Patience had left Bedford Square.

"How so?"

"Lord Holstrom put forth the investment as my backing against Povolti. Not only do I find myself without funds, but I also owe Holstrom." Sin was in the position he'd worked so hard against. His greatest fear—returning home with less than he departed with—stared him straight in the face, mocking him. "I am indebted to him and must fight again—and win—to repay my obligation."

"My father, he would…" She whispered quietly, knowing he would never accept her charity nor her father's assistance.

This was his wrong to right, not hers.

"No, Patience." Her name fell from his lips as if

he'd uttered it a thousand times before. "I will not call upon your charity."

"There must be something I can do to help," she pleaded.

Sin studied her profile in the mirror as she gently set the cloth beside the washbowl and turned back to face him. Her eyes sparkled in the glow from the wall sconce above her head.

"You owe me nothing." Sin pivoted to face her, done with the distance between them. "You can help me by returning home and keeping away from men like Holstrom and me. And places like the Albany."

Her head fell forward, and he regretted his stern tone. Hurting her was not his intention, yet there was no other way to keep her from trouble. Did she not recognize the danger she was in being alone in a gentleman's private chambers?

If they were discovered, Patience would never escape the scandal. It would mar her entire family, all while Sin was free to return to Brownsea Island without fear of the same following him. It was unjust, but the way of things in society.

"Please, Sin." She took the several steps toward him and grasped his hands. "If you are gravely injured or even killed, I would never forgive myself for allowing it to happen when I could have prevented it. I've wished for years that my father had found my mother before he did. Then, perhaps, she would have had other options. There must be something I can do to help. If not money, perhaps…"

"Knowing that you care is enough." He gently squeezed her hands and grinned. "I will take greater care before I fight again."

She scoffed. "Take better care? What do you mean by that?"

"I will practice. Mayhap I was too confident in my skill." Sin searched for a way to reassure her. "Watch other pugilists and learn their secrets."

"That will never work," she declared.

"Why ever not?"

"You would need to secure a trainer first, and you do not have the coin for that." She placed her hands on her hips and fell silent. He could almost see her thinking through all his options and coming to a solution. From her strained expression and pursed lips, it was not one she relished. "I will train you."

"Surely you jest!"

Her stare narrowed, piercing his as she took a step closer to him, her chin lifting as she got closer to keep her eyes focused on him. "Do you think me not skilled and sufficiently learned in the pursuit of pugilism?"

CHAPTER 9

PATIENCE ADJUSTED HER simple skirt and blouse as she stood before a building she hadn't entered in nearly six years. She'd forgone her usual mass of underpinnings and tight corset to allow herself freedom of movement and therefore increase her agility without hampering her ability to breathe.

And she would certainly need to breathe this day.

Glancing over her shoulder, Patience gave her maid a reassuring smile and nodded to her driver. Her father had nearly forbidden her from leaving their townhouse—and had strongly cautioned her against returning to Southlund's House.

The establishment held too many memories.

Both good and bad.

To this day, her father—despite owning a percentage of the club since his marriage to Ivory Bess—had never ventured through the doors. It had been the gift of a safe haven for Patience's mother, the Countess of Desmond, given upon the day she became betrothed to the Earl of Desmond.

Her father had said: "When you love another with all your heart, you are not only duty bound to give them your unconditional love, you also must make certain their heart is as full as yours."

It had been the way of things between her parents. Even though what filled her mother's heart eventually caused her demise. In short, her father had loved her mother so much he'd willingly given her something that would take her away from him...and their children.

Patience could not be angry with him for it. The Earl of Desmond hadn't been aware of his grave mistake when he gave his young love Southlund's House. Her father had only sought to make the woman he loved happy—there could never be fault in longing to make others happy.

Taking another deep breath, Patience ran her hands down the front of her skirts. It was a nervous gesture that did nothing to help with her clammy hands encased in her gloves. She longed to remove them and cast the finery aside; however, leaving the house without her stays and corset was nearly enough to give her father apoplexy. Leaving without her gloves would have pushed him over the edge and into utter madness.

There was nothing particularly special or noteworthy about the exterior of the building. It blended in nicely with the neighborhood, flanked by a merchant's shop on one side and an apothecary on the other. A tavern with several rooms for rent above sat across the street. The lane was quiet and well-maintained, thanks in part to Southlund's House's servants.

From this vantage point—safely outside and unable to see what the occupants were doing—Patience could nearly make herself believe that the building housed a regular, run-of-the-mill sparring facility where men—and some women—gathered to practice sporting activities of their choosing.

Fencing, archery, swordplay, and pugilism.

Yet, that was not the way of things. Men did not

seek out Southlund's House as a mere place to pursue their favored pastimes. This was not an establishment where gentlemen met their closest friends for a friendly fencing match to help keep their physique or while away their time before their evening entertainments.

No, Southlund's House was an elite club for men—and women—who sought careers in prizefighting. This was where her mother had trained when she was still the famed Ivory Bess and where the Countess of Desmond continued to train others after she'd wed and had children. The building before Patience housed rooms where she and her siblings had met with tutors while their mother worked with bare-knuckle boxers. The sound of fists against flesh was a common background accompaniment to their lectures and lessons on geography, arithmetic, and science.

Patience wanted to laugh—so as not to break down in tears—at the thought. Their schoolroom, staffed by the best London instructors, was in the back room of a pugilist club.

"Pardon, miss." A finely dressed gentleman stepped around her and entered Southlund's.

When the footman manning the door glimpsed her, his smile was broad and welcoming—an old friend surprised to see someone they'd thought to never encounter again.

"Lady Patience Lane?" The man rushed out of the building, his newest arrival forgotten instantly at the sight of her. "My, you have grown, my dear girl."

She couldn't help the genuine smile even as her throat tightened. "Mr. Caulfield. Elias." He was older, but the years had treated him well, with only a hint of grey around his ears and a slight thickening at his middle.

Mr. Elias, as they called him, had greeted them each time they arrived with her mother. He'd ordered them meals from the tavern kitchen across the street when they grew hungry, and her mother trained late into the evening, and he read her stories until she fell asleep when her mother worked late into the night.

"It is lovely to see you again." Patience embraced Mr. Elias without a second thought. An adored man who'd been closer to her than any servant at Marsh Manor. "I did not think to see you here today."

"And I cannot believe my own eyes that you are standing before me," he replied, his stare raking her from head to toe. "How long has it been? Three, no, four years?"

"Closer to five." Patience remembered the final time she'd spoken to Mr. Elias. It had been the afternoon of her mother's funeral at Marsh Manor. He'd come to give his best to her family. "How is Mrs. Caulfield?"

A coy grin broke across the man's face, making him appear the child who'd stolen the pie from the cooling window. "She is fine, fine indeed. About ready to have another babe."

"Another?" Patience asked.

"Oh, we haven't spoken in some time, after all." He stood straighter, his shoulders back and his chin high. "This will be our third child so far. Two boys. Hoping for a wee girl with this babe."

"The grandest of congratulations, Mr. Elias, from my family and me," Patience said with a light laugh, her downcast mood from moments before melting away. "I am certain you are a superb father."

Mr. Elias blushed, and his eyes widened. "Where are my manners? Do come in…" His words trailed off as if he realized he'd made a grave error in judgment. "Are you here to come inside, my lady?"

Patience pushed down her unease and turned to give her maid a quick wave, letting her know that all was as it should be. "Yes, Mr. Elias."

With a bright smile and a flourish of his arm, Mr.

Elias stepped back to allow her entrance. "It is our pleasure to have you return to Southlund's House. The place has not been the same in the time since"—His voice trembled—"your family has been away."

As if the Earl of Desmond and his children had been away on holiday and not grieving the loss of a wife and mother. It was a *holiday* Patience had never expected to return from.

Patience's chest tightened as she stepped across the threshold, and Mr. Elias allowed the door to close behind them, blocking the hazy morning sun. Closing her eyes, she gave herself permission to experience the sensations of being in a place that was once so familiar to her. The good memories, as well as the bad ones, washed over her again. The pungent odor of cigar smoke hung heavily in the air, tickling her throat. The clashing of foils and cheers of support drifted from one of the sparring rooms near the back of the building.

Instead of sorrow and pain, Patience's heart swelled to return to a place that had meant so much to her mother. It had been her mother's sanctuary, and Patience's second home for much of her life. The draw to return had always been strong, but easily deniable. She despised the sport that had taken her mother from her, and loving and longing for the place that had perpetuated the loss was illogical.

The logical track would have been to demand that her father close Southlund's House, selling the property, thus forgetting it had ever been so entangled in Patience's childhood.

"Are you only here to have a look about, or will you be sparring?"

"Actually…" She glanced sideways to gauge the man's reaction to her next words. "I will be training a prizefighter."

"Training? A fighter?" Mr. Elias fought to rein in his excitement. "Oh, Lady Patience, that is fine news.

Since your mother, bless her soul, left us, there have not been many female fighters attending Southlund's. And I had heard you were speaking out against the sport…"

"I was grieving my mother." If she'd succeeded in her mission or demanded the club be shut down, Mr. Elias would have needed to seek other employment, and his family would have suffered. Not as much as Patience and her siblings, but having one's income stripped away could devastate a man. "Has a new boxer arrived this morning?"

Part of her hoped St. Seville didn't show up at the allotted time and place. She could return home as if none of this had happened. Forget the earl and her rash offer to assist him. What had provoked her the night before?

She'd been lulled by their private moment in his chambers as she'd brazenly stepped forward to cleanse his wounds. Her skin against his. Her eyes meeting his. They'd both been caught off guard by her determination to see him to his room and make certain he was well.

Her bold actions had surprised her so utterly she'd quickly departed after securing his word that he would meet her at Southlund's House the following morning to start his proper education in the art of pugilism.

And it was an art.

She had forgotten what it felt like to be around fighters, to watch them perform.

"I cannot say, my lady," Mr. Elias said with a shake of his head. "I only arrived on duty moments before your arrival. However, I did pass a gathering in the back room. Perhaps your new fighter awaits you there."

Once St. Seville was surrounded by a few of England's foremost bare-knuckle boxers, he would truly note the importance of other skills, not only brute strength.

Was her offer to train him partly for selfish reasons?

Certainly, Patience wanted St. Seville—in the light of day he was once again St. Seville, not Sin—to save his lands and people. This was something she'd been unable to do for her own family. She wanted him to repay his debt to Holstrom and escape the clutches of both him and Coventry.

She needed to help him because, without her, he would fail and likely face far more serious injuries in his attempts in the ring.

But the truth was, she always wanted to be near him, despite there being no reason for their continued acquaintance. He was in London to do the one thing Patience loathed. So why had she not washed her hands of him and simply walked away? Kept herself separate from the sport that had caused her family such overwhelming loss and grief.

Patience had learned she was many things since her mother's death: strong, independent, determined. But now, selfish?

"I can see myself in." Patience gave the man another quick embrace and started for the hall that led to the back training room.

Everything from the burgundy carpeting to the dark wood walls was the same. As she turned down the hall, Patience knew she'd find the club's row of victors—as they called it. An entire hallway lined with portraits of pugilists, fencers, and archers who'd gained their training at Southlund's and had gone on to excel in their chosen sport. How many times had she sprinted down this exact hall, caught her toe on the loose carpet and fallen head over tail causing all sorts of scrapes and scratches? Over two dozen—and blaming her youthful follies on the carpeting was a ruse. She'd relished sneaking out of their townhouse after slipping on her elder sister's boots. They were not the tiny, childish half boots Patience was forced to wear, but more like those favored by the fancy women who promenaded in the park.

She kept her stare straight ahead, not lingering in the hall as she passed men departing the sparring rooms. If she paused for even a second, Patience knew she'd been drawn to a certain portrait that held a special place of honor on the wall. Bordered by a frame of gilded gold, her mother's image would stare back at her—her bare fists held high, her feet in the pugilist's stance, and her eyes alight with joy. There were many firsts since her mother's death that Patience was prepared to face today but the image of Ivory Bess was not one of them.

"Do not look. Keep moving. You are nearly there," she mumbled as she counted her steps, the fine hairs on the back of her night rising.

"Lady Patience?"

She stumbled to a halt, and her eyes met her mother's in the portrait on the wall. It was thirty-two strides to the end of the hallway. She'd only managed twenty-five, which meant there was no avoiding the sight of Ivory Bess.

The eyes staring back at her, a mix of merriment and determination, were mirror images of Patience's greyish blue orbs. Anger twisted at her stomach. Even though the image held no color, Patience knew her mother had a single red rose pinned to the strap of her bodice. It was the main reason her father had issued the command to have the thorny bushes below Patience's and Merit's bedchamber windows removed. It reminded them all of what they'd lost. She couldn't take the sight any longer and glanced away, blinking several times.

But they remained. It was one of the commands she'd fought her father on. Her hands clenched at the thought of her mother's lovely roses being pulled from their beds and discarded.

"My lord." Patience brought her gaze from the well-worn carpet, surprised to find she was looking at Sin. Dressed in loose trousers with his linen shirt lying open at his throat and his hair hanging free about his shoulders, he appeared the pirate she'd first mistaken him for. "Hmmm, you have arrived. And early."

"Yes, well, you said I had one chance, and I am not a man to squander an opportunity." He turned away from her toward the wall. "This is your mother?"

"Was." The single words came on an exhale. "That *was* my mother."

"She will never stop being your mother, despite her passing," he mused, keeping his stare on the wall.

"True, but I prefer to remember her differently."

"How so?"

"As a woman who loved her family above her sport," Patience snapped, her anger pushing past the pain of being at Southlund's House again. "I mean, I wish to remember her when she was healthy—appeared healthy, at least—before her mind was so easily confused and her limbs refused to obey."

His brow furrowed and he faced her. "Why did you bid me meet you here instead of another club if it would cause you such anguish?"

"Because—" She hadn't admitted this to anyone, and only a few members knew. "My father, and each of us children, owns a portion of Southlund's House, though none of us have been here in years. You do not have the funds to train at another club, and I was certain you would not allow me to pay for your training. At Southlund's, we can work without a fee."

"It is now I who cannot understand *you*, my lady. Coming back here, though it causes you no small amount of anguish…" he said with a stiff bow. "I am forever in your debt."

"Oh, do not fall all over yourself thanking my selflessness," she retorted. "As with everything, nothing is without a cost." She quieted as a pair of gentlemen passed them in the hall, one glancing over his shoulder to get a better look at Patience. "I have several conditions before we begin."

If St. Seville were rattled or leery in response to her announcement, he was quick to hide it with a tentative smile. "I would expect nothing less, my lady."

Patience shook her head. "First off, do not call me *my lady* or *Lady Patience* while at Southlund's House."

"What am I to call you?" he asked, as if appalled by her command.

"Patience will do."

"And what is your second condition, Patience?" he asked.

"That was not my first condition, my lord," she countered. "My first condition is that you are to listen and heed my advice…at all times."

Part of her longed to examine her motives for adding *at all times* and not merely stating while they were training. The sudden stiffness in his posture told her that he wondered the same.

"I think I can agree to that readily enough." He shrugged and turned back to her mother's portrait as if her first condition weren't overly troubling. "Next?"

Patience swallowed past the lump that had formed in her throat, knowing if he were to find fault with any of her conditions, this would be the one. "We train, you win your freedom from Holstrom, and stop boxing. Find another way to secure the funds needed to save your family."

"You cannot be serious," he growled.

"I most certainly am, my lord."

"And how do you propose I save my family and lands?"

It was Patience's turn to shrug. "We shall find a way."

"We?" he questioned.

"If I am the reason you are to give up pugilism as a career choice, then isn't it also my duty to make certain I assist you in finding another way to support your estate?" She'd gone over and over this discussion in her head a hundred times since she departed the Albany the previous night. He had to accept her help—and her conditions. He was not the first lord to find himself on the brink of financial ruin. How did those men return from the precipice? Putting his life in danger was not the answer, for his people would be ruined if he failed. "Do you agree?"

His brow rose in question. "To your condition or your reasoning?"

"Both, I would presume," she replied, really glancing at her mother's portrait for the first time, immediately regretting her weakness. The sight of her mother just before the prize match in which her father had spotted her for the first time brought tears to Patience's eyes. "But it is only my condition you must agree to at the moment."

"You have led me to believe I have no chance of besting other prizefighters without your assistance," he said. "So, truly, I have no option but to agree to any condition you set forth."

"Very true," she said, glancing down to cover the pain she suspected was evident in her eyes at being at Southlund's again. St. Seville was a force of a man, yet he gave in easily to her demands. At any other time, Patience would have been thrown off guard by his ready acquiescence. "This way to the sparring ring."

She didn't wait for his reply, but pushed past him and moved in the direction of the boxing room.

"That cannot be your only two conditions, my lady!" he called, hurrying behind her.

"How quickly you break my first rule." A hint of true laughter rose in her tone. "There is only one final thing, and I cannot think you will deny me it after agreeing to the other two," Patience threw over her shoulder as she rounded the corner into the sparing room. Thankfully, there was but one man using the area, and he was only standing against the far wall.

St. Seville caught up with her as she halted several feet into the room.

"What is the final condition?"

"Tell me why they call you Sin." It was likely the condition that piqued her interest the most. Certainly, it was a shortened version of his first name, Sinclair, but a name like Sin did not come without some story—or without some truth behind it.

Each of her demands came with their own motivation. First and foremost, Patience was acutely concerned that Holstrom, and possibly Coventry, was taking severe advantage of Sin. Both for their own gains. Next, Patience loathed the thought of a fighter being harmed when she could have helped.

Lastly, he was handsome as *sin*.

Never had Patience met a man who captured her notice so fully…and as the daughter of an earl, Patience had gained the acquaintance of nearly every eligible lord in all of England. Every rogue, rake, and scoundrel of worth had been presented to her during her three Seasons. None had left any lasting impression, only disdain and revulsion. Sometimes both at once.

"There is no grand meaning behind the name, but if that is your final condition, I readily agree." He moved farther into the room and pulled his white linen shirt over his head, revealing his chiseled chest and broad, muscled shoulders.

"Oh, I am certain there is a titillating tale behind the name," Patience muttered, thankful that Sin was far enough away that he didn't hear her words or the longing behind them. She crossed her arms over her blouse to hide the hardening peaks of her nipples as her cheeks flushed with heat. "Mayhap I am in need of *conditions* for this bargain, as well."

CHAPTER 10

SIN TOOK HIS place at the side of the ring where Patience had bidden him to wait—and watch—as she demonstrated a defense maneuver that she purported would have saved him from his defeat the previous night. The man who'd been in the room when they entered was another trainer who worked with fighters at Southlund's House, and he kindly stepped in to work with Sin and Patience.

"It is called the Bess step," Patience instructed as she maneuvered into the common boxing stance. "First, you must know if your opponent favors his left or right side, and then you step away, duck, and twist. Yes, the footwork takes you away from your opponent; however, when you duck and twist back, your strength doubles due to your trajectory."

Patience signaled for her sparring partner to advance on her and demonstrated the move with a quick deftness he'd never be able to replicate. He couldn't take his eyes off her, yet, was too distracted to truly comprehend the maneuver she attempted to teach him. The lithe movements of her body, the confidence in her voice, and the way she grounded and balanced her frame surprised Sin—in a delightful way.

As soon as he'd removed his shirt, she'd grasped the hem of her skirt and tucked it into her waistband. Sin hadn't known what he expected when she'd offered to instruct him, but Patience physically being in the ring hadn't so much as crossed his mind.

He'd thought, perhaps, that she would stand to the side and shout moves at him while he sparred with another fighter. But, no, she'd entered the area with as much confidence as a seasoned boxer.

Her skill was that of an expert. It had only served to spark his jealousy as she instructed him to wait and watch while she jabbed, weaved, and parried every move her opponent attempted. Sin hadn't been allowed to show her what he had mastered in his years on Brownsea Island as she led him through the basics of bare-knuckle boxing. They were all techniques Sin was aware of but had never paid particular attention to thinking himself strong enough to ignore true technique. Even today, he was having a difficult time remaining focused on anything but the lace of her stockings and the way her blouse, damp with perspiration, clung to her bosom. She'd removed her gloves again, and Sin remembered all too clearly the soft touch of her skin against his battered face and neck.

In the last several hours, she'd barely glanced in his direction as she focused on her movements, not even noticing the men who'd come to watch—and then left once the novelty of seeing a woman spar waned.

Sin had underestimated her. Or perhaps he hadn't wanted to assume more than was proper. Even as the daughter of a famed prizefighter, Sin hadn't expected her to share the same level of expertise as her mother.

The heartache had been plain in her demeanor when they met in the hallway. As the time passed and she continued to demonstrate move after move, she'd relaxed, the tension leaving her. It had to be difficult for her to be here, after all these years. A place her mother frequented.

If he'd known that she planned to bring him to such a familiar place, would he have argued against it or turned down her offer of help?

"Did you see what I did with my last movement?" she asked, glancing over her shoulder. "He had all his weight on his front left foot after throwing a jab. I ducked to the right and came around with a solid punch just below the ribs. Throwing him off balance and causing him to fall to a knee."

Sin nodded, and the fighters reset.

He'd had no other option but to agree to her conditions, and truly, he needed her help, and she had offered it. If he'd said no, he would have continued his plight, and she would have returned to her life and society.

Never again would their paths have crossed.

Perhaps that fate would have been far wiser than the course they were currently set upon—together.

Sin hadn't wanted to walk away from Patience. Every moment with her near only solidified that in his mind.

"I think St. Seville has seen enough for one morning, and it is time to see if he's learned anything from our demonstration," Patience announced, stepping forward to clasp her opponent's hand. "Daniels, thank you for remaining to assist the earl and me."

"It was my pleasure, Lady Patience," the man said, ducking his head. "Your mother inspired my love of pugilism, and it has been an honor to teach at Southlund's House." He turned to Sin. "My lord. I do hope to work with you again."

"As do I," Sin grunted, gaining a sideways glance from Patience. The woman should be satisfied that he hadn't growled at Daniels. The instructor was obviously smitten with Patience and had been afforded the opportunity to touch her in ways that made Sin want to challenge the man—but not in the ring, with pistols at dawn. "Thank you for your time."

She reminded him of the island fishwives whose strong, capable hands knotted ropes as if they were singlehandedly responsible for hauling their husbands from between the teeth of the storms, returning them safely to shore and their families. Patience had the confident fists of a woman who would never lose.

The instructor hurried from the room, leaving them blessedly alone for the first time since their brief conversation in the hall.

"Are you ready?" she asked, gesturing for him to take his place.

She could not be serious, Sin mused. A slip of a woman in the ring with a man of his size? He'd witnessed her skill up against Daniels, but certainly she realized one well-landed punch from him could do much damage.

He—at nearly eighteen stones and well over six feet in height—was to fight against a woman of no more than eight stones?

Those facts notwithstanding, he didn't want to fight her—he longed to hold her…the closer the better. Smell the floral scent of her dark hair, stroke her creamy skin until his fingertips teased at her collarbone. Stare down into her upturned face as he held her tight…

She must have noticed his hesitation because she smirked and tilted her head slightly. "You truly do believe sheer size and strength are all that is needed."

If the last several hours had taught Sin anything, it was that prizefighting took more skill and expertise than being blessed with an overabundance of muscle. "What if I unwittingly harm you?"

She outright laughed, threw her head back as the sound bounced off the walls. "You still have much to learn, my lord."

"So you keep informing me." Sin couldn't help his smile as he joined her on the sparring floor. "I am your pupil to shape and instruct, Lady Patience."

Sin bowed grandly, and they both laughed again.

Setting his feet in the aggressive stance she'd shown him, Sin waited for her to call a start to their match.

Another hour passed swiftly as he attempted to best Patience; however, more often than not, it was her punches and jabs that landed solidly, and Sin's that were met by nothing but air as she expertly ducked and dodged his every attempt. Her every movement was smooth like the trickle of the steam that ran from one side of Brownsea Island to the other and out to sea once more. Patience was calculated, and he admired her tendency to think ahead of his next move.

Never in his wildest meanderings had he thought to find himself fighting against a woman—let alone Patience. Sin didn't want to admit that there was a certain elegance to their practice match, almost as if they were in some sort of dance they both knew, seamlessly going through the motions, their bodies and minds in alignment with one another.

They came close again, and their labored breaths mingled.

Sin's eyes drifted closed for a brief moment, savoring the closeness as their bodies gave off heat from their exertion.

It was all the opportunity Patience needed, the opening he'd allowed her, and her fist collided with his jaw, sending a wave of pain up to his eyes and down his neck.

He stumbled back and dropped to one knee, his eyes leveling on her uncovered legs.

"Oh, my lord," Patience yelped and dropped her hands to her sides. "I did not mean to—"

"Hit me so hard?" He shook his head to clear his

focus—hoping to dispel his chagrin. First he'd been easily bested by Povolti and now by Patience. "It is not your fault, I was distracted, and my attention slipped. A hard-learned lesson, as it were."

She knelt beside him, and Sin sank back to the floor.

"Let me see how bad it is." She reached forward and gently put her fingers on his jawline, tilting his head from side to side as she scrutinized where he'd been hit. "I do not think you will suffer a bruise, though I cannot see through your facial hair. Ice would help stop any swelling or future aches."

Her touch lingered on his jaw as if she needed a longer look to confirm her words.

"I will be fine," he said, waving off her concern. "It did not hurt overmuch, only startled me."

A clock sounded from somewhere in the building…once, twice, three times, and Patience stiffened, her hand falling away from his face, grazing his arm as it fell to her side. A red-hot heat coursed up his arm as if she'd touched him with fire.

The warmth that had surrounded them fled as she pushed to her feet, holding out her hand for Sin to take. He willingly grasped it, and she assisted him to stand. She was stronger than he'd ever imagined.

"It is growing late," she sighed. "You must be exhausted and hungry."

As if on cue, his stomach let out a groan. "My morning meal was the last I ate."

"My father will be expecting me home, as well." She paused, glancing around the room. "We can meet here again tomorrow if that is suitable. You did very well today."

"You knocked me from my feet," he scoffed. "It would be in my best interest to gain as much practice as you offer." He was exhausted, the exertions of the last couple of hours tiring him far more than it should have.

"Yes, but you lasted longer than I expected. With time and training, you will improve. We shall meet at the same time until you are called to fight again." She kept her eyes on the floor, but managed to glance up at him from beneath her lowered lashes. It was the first time she'd ever employed the coy glance that so many young misses favored. Yet, Sin didn't believe she meant it to tease him—or even gain his notice. "You did very admirably."

Bloody hell. The woman had held his notice since the night he fled her home in nothing but his breeches and boots. He wanted nothing more than to have her hand caressing his jawline again, or several more minutes with her kneeling beside him in the ring—just the two of them.

"Tell me, my lord," Patience said, moving to untuck her skirts and letting them cascade to the floor. "Have you heard from Lord Holstrom? Has he arranged another match for you?"

The last person on Sin's mind was Holstrom, which would not do if he sincerely meant to rescue his lands from ruination. He needed to reassert his goals; however, the one person who could help him achieve those objectives was the woman distracting him from his responsibilities in the first place.

"He sent a note round this morning." Sin fell silent as he glanced back at her before slipping his shirt back over his head, something akin to hunger shining in her eyes. "Five days hence, in the evening, off Queen Street in Seven Dials."

"That will allow you some time to train further." Her face etched with concern, much as it had the evening before in his chambers. "That is a most dangerous area, my lord. Even my father will not venture far into such unsavory neighborhoods."

He was familiar enough with London and the surrounding boroughs to know the risk posed when journeying to places like Seven Dials in the West End; however, there was little alternative. He needed the prize purse, and he couldn't jeopardize his association with Holstrom by denying the fight. The man's note had been a strongly worded threat: Sin owed him a debt, and Holstrom *would* collect.

"The location may not be ideal, but the purse is more than sufficient to cover the risks involved."

Her brows drew down, and she crossed her arms. "How much?"

"Fifteen thousand pounds. I can repay Holstrom and"—Sin couldn't admit he intended to continue fighting, despite his promise—"it will allow me to send money home to my family."

He ignored the regret that threatened to distract him.

Still, the amount was far from what was needed to bring his coffers back to sustainable levels.

Sin slipped on his coat, and her stare landed on the golden *W* still pinned to his lapel.

Patience's mouth pulled into a thin line, and her glare hardened.

"Why do you take such offense to Coventry and his lot?" Sin remembered Coventry's words of warning against further association with Patience or her father; however, he hadn't spoken overly ill of the family. Patience was a bit of a hoyden with her idealistic notions. Sin would be proud if his younger sister, Juliette, took half the initiative Patience did when she set her mind to something. "He is not a vile man."

"I never said he was," she retorted, turning to grasp her handbag. "Though he and his men—with their illicit club and debauched natures—will be the downfall of all society. Where shall a proper young miss find a suitable, loyal, honest, and steadfast husband?"

Did she jest or were her words spoken with all seriousness? Sin thought her true feelings likely lay somewhere in the middle.

"So, your anger with Coventry and the Wicked Earls' Club is for the benefit of all womankind?" Either Patience was the most selfless lady in all of England, or her words were meant to distract him from her real purpose. "And what of you and your search for a husband?"

Her eyes widened in panic, and she placed her palm against her chest. "It is not I who I am concerned with, my lord," she said. "It is the less sound of mind— perhaps we should call it those lacking common sense— who would fall prey to the scoundrels and find themselves forever attached to a husband only interested in his own…pleasure." The word *pleasure* came on a hushed hiss.

"You do not give young misses enough credit," he countered. "I can assure you my sister would never fall prey to such a man."

"Sometimes it is not up to the lady who she weds." Patience turned pensive, and Sin wondered if she faced a fate such as that in the near future. "What if the man promised you enough funds to see your estate once again a wealthy one? Would you turn down the match?"

What if someone stepped forward with the promise of solving all his problems? Could he turn down such an offer to save his sister, all the while dooming his estate? His chest ached to think that one day it might come to that exact decision. Sin was determined not to allow his situation to become so dire.

"I would certainly not turn down a suitable match to a gentleman who loved my sister, especially if the affection was mutual. But you cannot cast doubt on such a marriage just because the St. Seville estate would see gains." Sin stumbled over each word, not as positive about his decision in such a situation as his replied proclaimed. "Besides, Juliette is likely to find a match in Dorset and never meet the likes of any of Coventry's horde."

"I will meet you here on the morrow, and I insist on accompanying you to Seven Dials." Her sudden change in topic was meant to throw Sin off track, which it did.

"You are not coming to the fight," he argued. Southlund's House was one thing. But Seven Dials? Grown men were not guaranteed safety in such neighborhoods. The risks for a woman were only compounded.

"What was my first condition?" She set her fists on her hips.

"I will listen and heed your advice," he mumbled. "But you cannot mean to journey to such an unsavory area. You said so yourself, even your father is hesitant to travel there."

She smirked, and he realized she held the upper hand. "It will not be difficult to secure the directions to the fight, and you will thank me for attending if things end as your last match did."

He shook his head, vigorously, but suspected further argument would fall on deaf ears. "You must think of your reputation."

"Women attend prizefights regularly. And besides, pugilism is not a taboo sport in society, it is widely accepted, and this will hardly be my first—or hundredth—fight. My mother took me along to many of her pupils' matches." She started for the front of the club. "This will be no different for me."

Sin clenched his jaw to stop from smiling. At some point, her way of throwing comments over her shoulder as if what she said was how things would be—and he need only nod and follow—had become endearing and expected, not heavy-handed as most of society thought.

Yet, unlike his association with Holstrom, Sin was in a position to deny her.

CHAPTER 11

PATIENCE COULDN'T HELP but smile, nor did she attempt to hide the bounce in her step as she alighted from her carriage and started toward the door to her family's townhouse. There had been so many emotions—grief, loss, heartache—coursing through her when she arrived at Southlund's House. She'd despaired at the thought of making it through an entire morning of training without breaking down in tears before the earl. However, she'd done it. The hours had flown by as if they were only minutes.

Caution had been cast aside as she was wont to do, and she'd taken a risk.

And, perhaps because of it, she returned home with a newfound sense of contentment. A weight had lifted from her shoulders. The pain of losing her mother still burrowed deep in her heart; however, something akin to…hope?…blossomed, as well. It was shocking that a few hours spent at Southlund's House could cause such a transformation within her.

She'd faced a huge hindrance she'd avoided since her mother's death—with Sin by her side, though he wasn't aware of it—and she'd survived. Thrived even.

Southlund's House belonged to her and her family, and Patience had proven, even if only to herself, that she could return to the place her mother cherished, find meaning and understanding in the sport her mother loved, even if her goal in life was to end what her mother held so dear. She'd pledged to herself and her family that she would never venture into the building again, that she'd spend her life until her final breath, speaking out on the dangers of pugilism. If her mother had known the risks and ailments she faced, would she still have loved the sport?

Patience was uncertain. Her mother had always been a woman free from the oppression that many people were crushed under due to their social class— she'd been raised in the poorest area of London and taken up a career no society lady would ever dare. The Countess of Desmond hadn't allowed anything to hold her back. Perhaps Patience was more akin to her mother than she'd realized.

If nothing else, she'd been overwhelmed by her mother's presence in the large building. She'd even found that she still relished the physical activity pugilism demanded of her body. The give and take. The side-to-side movements. The exertion necessary to tire your opponent.

The hours had passed with a swiftness that surprised Patience as she and Daniels sparred, leaving Sin to stand at the edge of the ring and watch until it was his turn. And he'd been a formidable partner, to be certain, yet once she began her sparring with Sin, she'd found herself transported back to their time in his private chambers. The way his bare skin had rippled under her touch. She'd been as distracted as he claimed to be when she threw the crushing blow to his jaw. She hadn't meant to injure him, and she'd been going easy with her jabs and punches the entire match. She knew he'd done the same, both frightened of harming one another.

And she would do it all over again tomorrow…and with any luck, the next five days until Sin was called to Seven Dials. She would push him, demand he train hard before having some rest before the fight.

Her heart still raced with exhilaration. She'd been so preoccupied with it all that she'd utterly forgotten to inquire after his moniker—Sin.

"Good day, Lady Patience," Donaldson, the Desmond butler greeted, holding the door open for her.

"Good day to you, too." If the servant were taken aback by Patience's jovial mood and appearance, he did not let on. "Wonderful day, is it not?"

"Of course, my lady." He hesitated for a moment before closing the door. "Your father, along with Lord Valor and Mr. Merit Lane await you in the study."

"Await me?" The bounce in her step faltered. She'd known her brothers were due to return to town any day, but why would they seek an audience with her immediately and not wait until supper? Or pester her in her room? Their mutual relationship was far less formal than being *summoned* to the study. "Whatever for?"

"I have not been apprised of that; however, I was instructed to send you directly to them when you arrived home."

"Thank you." Patience debated seeking out her chambers to change her gown before meeting with her father and brothers but decided against it. If something were amiss, Patience wanted to know with all due haste. And if she'd done something to garner their irritation or anger, their ire would only increase if she dawdled. Never the less, she was overjoyed to see her brothers, no matter the reasons for their impatience. "I will attend them straight away."

"I will let the housekeeper know to bring tea," the servant said with a smile.

Patience glanced in the hall mirror on the way to

her father's study, pausing to inspect her hair. Several long tendrils had worked their way free of the knot at the back of her neck and hung over her shoulders. Her skin glowed from physical activity, but beyond that, it was only her simple skirts and plain blouse that indicated that she'd been up to anything abnormal. Her father knew she had departed that morning to visit Southlund's House. She had no reason to hide that fact, and if he asked, she'd inform him that she was instructing the Earl of St. Seville in the finer art of bare-knuckle boxing. Her driver and maid had accompanied her to the club, as was proper, though Patience need not share that she'd bidden her companion to await her in the carriage. Nothing untoward had occurred, at least not that morning at the club.

And her father had no knowledge of her whereabouts the previous night, but she was fairly certain he'd find fault and scandal in her visiting Sin's private chambers at the Albany. But there was little chance he knew of that unless her driver had tattled on her.

Patience doubted that, as well. The servant would surely be fearful of losing his position if her father ever learned of the escapade, not that she ever wished to jeopardize someone's position within her household. Allowing a lady to go gallivanting about town, entering a private men's-only lodging house…the gossips would have fodder for years if they learned of Patience's goings-on.

Thankfully, she'd reached a certain level among the *ton* where no one would pay her the slightest mind even if she arrived at the opera or Vauxhall in nothing but her underpinnings and stockings. Perhaps her standing as a societal outcast came in useful from time to time, as long as her known activities did not stray too far into scandalous territory.

Her footsteps made no sound as she traversed the

hall to her father's study.

She lifted her clenched fist—a tweak of pain from her morning's sparring traveled through her fingers and into her hand—and knocked on the closed door.

"Enter," her father called, his voice sounding far away, distracted. It wasn't uncommon for him, and had truly become the norm since her mother's death.

Present but not altogether there.

Alive but not living.

Hearing but not listening.

The Earl of Desmond, once a loving, nurturing father, could rarely be bothered to attend to his children. The change had been glaringly obvious directly after his wife's passing; however, now, it was like he'd always been as such. Many times, Patience thought he only delivered her pamphlets to be out of her sight.

Patience entered the room to see her father in his usual place behind his desk and Merit and Valor taking up space on the two chaise lounges close to the hearth, leaving Patience to choose from the two straight-backed, hard-seated chairs before her father.

"Good day, Patience." Her father didn't bother to lift his stare from the papers on his desk. "Do take a seat."

Patience glanced at her elder brothers, hoping one would take pity on her and allow her a place on a lounge, but neither would meet her stare as they remained silent. Her warm greeting died on her lips.

"I shall stan—"

"Sit." Her father's command echoed in the room, and both her brothers turned sideways glances at her. "There is something troubling I'd like to discuss with you."

"With Merit and Valor present?" she squeaked, her bright mood fading quickly.

He sighed, finally bringing his head up to meet her stare. "After what I heard today, I am certain your brothers being present for this conversation is the least of your worries."

His words held a hard edge that Patience hadn't heard in years. She was torn between being excited that some semblance of her old father had returned and leery of what he'd heard and what he had to say. Nevertheless, when he gestured to the chair before him, Patience sank into it, the stiff, straight back biting into her shoulder blades.

"I received a very interesting correspondence this morning."

"Oh," Patience said. "I do hope it was interesting in a positive way."

Her father cleared his throat before continuing. "Patience, would you agree I give you freedoms not allowed other women of your tender age?"

"Yes." Her chest tightened. "And I am very grate—"

"Would you say that with that freedom there is an unspoken agreement between us?" His eyes narrowed, and Patience noticed, perhaps for the first time, how he'd aged in the last several years. "And, in turn for you respecting society's rules for young ladies, I agreed to distribute your pamphlets."

"Of course," she said hesitantly. "Is this about going to Southlund's House this morning?"

"Did you inform me of your intent to visit the club?"

"Yes."

"Then that is in keeping with our unspoken agreement, is it not?" he asked, his voice quiet and unhurried.

"Y—es," she conceded.

He folded his arms on the desk in front of him. "Mayhap you should ponder where you've been recently that you have not told me about."

Patience's heart skipped a beat, and she clutched

her hands tightly in her lap as she made a show of thinking though her movements over the last several days. The truth was, she'd been a couple of places—Bedford Square, the Albany, and Sin's private chambers—she hadn't told her father about. And she had no plans to admit to them now.

"Did you accost Lady Holstrom in her own home?" he seethed.

His seriousness only served to incite deep chuckles from Merit and Valor.

Patience pivoted in her seat, her narrowed stare pinning Merit and then Valor, quieting them instantly. They might be the elder siblings—and male—but they'd learned long ago not to poke fun at their youngest sibling.

"No, Father." Patience kept her voice level. "I did not accost Lady Holstrom, I only attempted—"

"Lord Holstrom has proclaimed the opposite." He fell silent and stared at his desk.

Belatedly, Patience realized he was rereading a correspondence.

"He also informed me that you and he were embroiled in a verbal altercation in the hall outside his office…at the same soirée."

Patience snorted. "I would not go so far as to call it a verbal altercation."

The earl's fist landed sharply on his desk, halting Patience's words. "I must say, I am inclined to believe Holstrom."

"Father, this is preposterous," Patience fumed, leaning over the desk that separated them, her stare begging her father to disregard whatever Holstrom—the scoundrel—had written. "I merely wanted a word with the lord, and he did not favor a meeting with me." He held up his hand to silence her but Patience would not be quieted, not if it meant a man such as Holstrom gained the upper hand in her household. "If you do not believe me, inquire the truth of the matter from the Earl of St. Seville."

"St. Seville?" her father mumbled. "What does he have to do with any of this?"

"He happened upon Holstrom and me in the hall." Patience sat back, crossing her arms. "I am certain he will tell you that what I speak is truth."

"What makes you think I would take St. Seville's word on a matter as grave as this?"

"I cannot think why you would believe Lord Holstrom over your daughter; however, here we are."

Her retort did as expected, causing her father to raise from his seat with frustration. "It is not only his concerns with you at the soirée, Patience. I can overlook such trivial instances as that."

Patience was suddenly alert and wary. He thought her actions at the soirée trivial even though she'd deceived him into believing she hadn't brought her pamphlets to the gathering?

"Then I must confess, I am uncertain why you are vexed with me."

He returned to his chair. "Where were you last evening?"

"At what time, specifically?"

"Do not play coy, Patience," he thundered, causing both Merit and Valor to spring from their lounges. "I will only ask the question one more time. Where were you last evening?"

If the information were coming from Holstrom, then the only place he knew of her being was Bedford Square. He couldn't know she'd returned Sin to his lodging—and accompanied him inside. Could he?

Having her trailed wasn't something Lord Holstrom seemed prone to do.

However, having Sin followed after the prizefight seemed at least plausible.

"I was at Bedford Square for a short time." It was

best to only admit the smallest of her infractions, especially if her father weren't any the wiser about her two evenings stationed outside the Albany and her even more scandalous time within the lodging house. "There was a match between two acclaimed pugilists. I was only there for a short time, and my driver accompanied me."

"I was unaware you were leaving the townhouse at all."

Patience wanted to tell him that he'd be much more informed if he exited his office with more regularity when he was home other than to find sleep and chaperone Patience to social gatherings, but she kept her mouth shut. Bringing him to anger would not benefit her in any way, and she still needed to slip from the house unnoticed for the upcoming fight in Seven Dials, not to mention it would be necessary for her to visit Southlund's House for further training. She could not risk having her father take a keener interest in her comings and goings.

It was best to make amends and promise that she'd not do anything so reckless again.

Her apology stuck in her throat, though. Outright lying to her father was something she'd immediately regret.

"I will do my best to keep you abreast of my plans in the future, Father." She lowered her head for good measure, hoping he took the gesture as resignation and not a means of hiding her face from his all too perceptive stare. There had been a time that a mere glance from her father would be enough for Patience to spill whatever secrets she held. Now was not the time to risk finding out if he still had the skill to draw information from her. "I am sorry if my actions caused you any trouble."

"For heaven's sake, girl," he sighed, the tension leaving him. "I love you to distraction"—an odd turn of phrase for her father to use—"and if anything or anyone harmed you, I would be adrift. You are my youngest, Patience, and your mother's favorite—"

"What?" Valor shouted with fake outrage.

"You jest, Father." Merit leapt to his feet; though, truly, neither man could be shocked at her father's words.

The pair was consistent and predictable if anything.

"If anything,"—her father's voice broke, and he swallowed before continuing—"if anything ever happened to you, your mother would never forgive me."

In moments such as this, Patience wondered if her father remembered that his countess was gone and not only just momentarily out of the room. Her heart ached all the more for the hurt he suffered each day. Yes, Patience had lost her mother—as had her siblings—but her father had lost the greatest love of his life. He'd never been common stock of nobility. No, the Earl of Desmond had proclaimed his love and adoration for Ivory Bess far and wide long before securing her as his wife. That love had produced five healthy, happy children.

"I will endeavor to remain above scandal and any hint of gossip, Father."

"Oh, fiddle-faddle, girl." The earl reclined in his seat and pinched the bridge of his nose. "I am not, and never have been, concerned with idle gossip. It is your safety that is paramount and of the utmost concern to me."

She stood and hurried around the desk to press a kiss to her father's cheek. He might shy away from any affection, but that did not mean Patience need do the same.

"I love you, Father," she whispered in his ear. "If there was one thing I learned from Mother, it was to avoid danger whenever possible." Of course, she'd also learned to step inside a punch when necessary, but there was no reason to remind her father of such lessons. "If there is nothing else, may I go?"

He waved his hand, his attention already focused on his work. "Yes, yes, yes and take your brothers with you. I am much too busy to have them going on and on about their time in the country."

She took in her brothers, their identical smiles turned in her direction and, without a doubt, Patience knew they were up to something. Though four years separated the men, they were nearly always found together as a pair. Where one went, the other followed. It didn't help matters much that in just the perfect lighting, Merit and Valor appeared more like identical twins than brothers of dissimilar ages. Something Patience suspected they'd used to their advantage many times.

"Come along." Patience sighed and hurried toward the study door. "I suppose I'd like to hear about the country house party you both attended."

The pair caught up with her in the hall as she made her way to the main stairs, flanking her on each side.

"We disagree. What you've been up to is far more entertaining than our silly house party," Merit whispered, slipping his hand through the crook of her arm.

"Yes, *dear* sister." Valor voiced, a tone or two too high for a gentleman. "We have it on good authority that Bedford Square is not the only place you *visited* last night."

Patience halted, turning to stare daggers at her two brothers. "Whom did you hear that from?"

Both shrugged with innocence, but it was Valor who spoke, "Does it matter?"

"It most certainly does," she retorted. Damnation, but Patience hadn't been careful at all. She hadn't kept an eye on who was around the Albany or if anyone paid her any particular mind. Apparently, she wasn't as unseen as she'd thought.

"Let us say that Holstrom isn't the only bloke keeping watch on you, Patience." Valor smirked and elbowed Merit.

"In fact," Merit picked up where Valor left off, "we have also been informed that there is to be another prizefight. And that you shall be in attendance."

How did the pair know anything about her plans? She'd only discovered the fight and set her course an hour prior.

"I am certain Father would delight in knowing where—and with whom—you will be spending your evening. However…" Valor's words trailed off as he tapped at his chin in thought.

"However, if you were to allow us to escort you to the match, then it would benefit all three of us," Merit finished triumphantly.

The devils were planning to blackmail her.

The scoundrels.

"How so?" Patience took a step back from her brothers.

"Well, you shall have chaperones"—He gestured between himself and Valor—"and we will make a pretty shilling if we hedge our coin on the right fighter. Father cannot reprimand you for your choice of evening entertainment if we accompany you."

Her muscles tensed with uncertainty and more than likely a healthy bit of disuse from her earlier activities. If she allowed the pair to accompany her, they would note her connection to Sin; however, if she denied them, her brothers would more than likely follow her anyway and possibly tattle on her to their father.

How could she arrive to collect Sin with Merit and Valor in tow?

The alternative was missing the pugilist match altogether, but she'd promised St. Seville she'd be there. And though she'd seen firsthand how much he'd improved after only one lesson, Patience shuddered to think of the fighter Sin would face with a prize as grand as fifteen thousand pounds.

Reluctantly, Patience nodded. "Very well, I will permit you to accompany me to the fight; however, what I do and whom I speak with is my business only. Neither of you"—She pinned both men with her hardest stare—"will even so much as utter a word about my activities to Father."

Merit slapped his thigh before clasping Valor on the back, both whooping with excitement.

"The pair of you are incorrigible," Patience huffed. "The fight is five days hence. Be ready at eight o'clock that evening to depart. Not a moment later."

The pair was free to join her during the ride to Seven Dials, but her other daily activities—and her time at Southlund's House—were hers alone…hers and Sin's. If things did not go as planned and Sin was again defeated, they would need find other means for gaining the funds to save his estate.

Though it had never interested her before, Patience wondered how substantial her dowry was and if her father would speak of it when asked. Certainly, matters would not become so dire; however, having the information would still her nerves. The next several days of training would be crucial.

With a reserved smile, she spun around, her skirts flaring around her ankles, and headed up the stairs, her step far more hesitant than a moment before.

CHAPTER 12

SIN EXITED SOUTHLUND'S House not long after noon to see that the early morning sun—a rarity in London or so he'd been told—had been overtaken by a layer of clouds that would no doubt bring with it evening drizzle that would likely turn to a downpour during the late-night hours. Thankfully, Sin had no plans for his evening except to find his bed—and perhaps write a letter to Juliette and his mother.

Rotating his shoulders brought a fresh wave of pain to his back. The endless hours of training were taking a hefty toll on him. How so many prizefighters managed to sustain a decade-long career in the ring was a mystery to Sin. He'd only been in London a short two weeks, and already, he was looking forward to returning home. Though he also longed for the day when there would be a reason to have Patience close without the need for sparring as a motive.

"The breeze carries the scent of rain, my lord," the lady of his thoughts mused, tucking a sack under her arm before glancing up at him. Her eyes matched the tumultuous clouds above—grey without a hint of their actual color, blue. She'd taken to arriving with the sack, hurriedly changing into her sparring gear before they entered the practice area at Southlund's. And at the end of her sessions, she'd transform herself once more from the daughter of Ivory Bess into a proper London lady.

Could it be that Patience struggled as he did? A war between who he was, who he wanted to be, and what necessity demanded of him? Did all those wage war within her, as well?

He had never found anything lacking in his life at Brownsea until the crushing weight of his empty coffers pushed him from the safety of the island. It was only then that he realized he'd need to discover who he was and what he wanted his life to hold. Had their recent association done the same for Patience, casting doubt on who she was and what fulfilled her?

Her brow furrowed in that way that Sin was becoming accustomed to of late. "Nightfall will come early, as well, I presume."

Such a mundane topic did nothing to cool Sin's heated skin from their hours of training; neither did the wind that rushed down the street, billowing her skirts around her ankles and pulling free his hastily tied cravat. He'd learned quickly that if he took overlong donning his own proper attire after Patience's lessons, she would slip from Southlund's House without him.

Not this day. He craved a few more moments with her, even if only to discuss the commonplace seasonal weather. Sin would be damned if he allowed her to escape into the early afternoon, only to hear from the footman at the door that Lady Patience "looked forward to another training session the following day" with little more than a nod as he departed.

The Desmond carriage waited at the curb as it had since the first time she'd bid him meet her at Ivory Bess's famed pugilist training house. Not far down the walk, in the other direction, waited the hackney driver who'd come to recognize Sin's patterns of late and waited outside the Albany as faithfully as his driver in Brownsea Island did.

Neither of them said their goodbyes or moved toward their waiting conveyances.

Could it be that Patience stalled, too?

"I find I have become rather inured to the gloomy weather in town," Sin offered.

"One must acclimate to survive, I fear," she replied with hesitation as if something weighed on her. They both fell silent and still. Sin was perfectly content allowing the world around them to keep moving: people scurrying to and fro, carriages pulled by overworked horses, a farmer pulling a cart loaded with winter fruit to the market, and men on horseback navigating the perilous thoroughfare.

It all happened around them, yet Sin, with Lady Patience by his side, was not a part of it all.

Her tense shoulders and clutched hands told him that she wanted to say something—and it was gravely important to her. It was the same with his younger sister Juliette when she'd gathered the courage to come to Sin's study at Brownsea to ask for permission to attend the village's annual Christmastide rout. She'd been only fifteen and still in the schoolroom at the time; however, Sin had not been able to deny her anything.

As he suspected, he would be unable to deny lady Patience her every request now.

He only prayed she did not mean to end their training sessions.

In the last few days, Sin had been so captured and enthralled during his time at Southlund's House with Patience, that he'd been able to cast from his mind all the secrets he held—and the lies to come. During their hours of training, he'd only wanted to please her, to show her his progress, and to see Patience's smirk of accomplishment at her successful tutelage.

"My lord," she mumbled, watching a cart rumble

past. "May I be so bold as to inquire about your plans for the rest of the day?"

His patience had paid off—tenfold—and Sin was quick to suppress his smile and ignore the way his stomach leapt with joy at just the sight of her. "You may."

"There is place I'd like to take you." She glanced at her waiting carriage, but Sin noted that her driver had yet to see that his mistress had exited the club, and so they remained unnoticed. Even the passing carriages on the street and the people on the walk paid them no mind. "I have not been in many years; however, it is still a location innately tied to my mother's world."

Sin knew how difficult it had been for Patience to enter Southlund's House again after her mother's death. Why would she punish herself again…for him?

"I have naught on my mind but finding my bed at the Albany, my lady."

Her gaze shifted to meet his. "I have pushed you hard."

Was that regret in her tone?

"No harder than was necessary, I assure you," he replied. Every muscle in his body ached, though Patience moved with the lithe grace of a woman who trained every day. "Please, tell me more about where we are going."

"Only if you allow me use of your hack." She nodded toward his waiting driver—not *his* driver, but a man paid each day to deliver him between the Albany, Southlund's House, and occasionally, the Wicked Earls' Club. "I fear my driver has been very obliging of late, but where I plan to take you today would give him— and my father—apoplexy for certain."

"Perhaps that is a reason we should not go." He tested her resolve. Though she had offered to train him, Sin couldn't help but fear that he'd asked a lot of her during their short acquaintance, and this might very well be too much for her to undertake. "Are you certain it is safe?"

Safe for your heart, he wanted to add.

Her physical safety was not in jeopardy, not when Sin was near. Just as he would do for his mother and sister, he would protect Lady Patience with his life if the situation demanded it.

He could not protect her from herself, however.

"Are you one to shy away from things because of how others will react?"

If her question had been a fist, Sin would have been knocked to the ground and left dazed and confused. It was something they had in common— neither held back due to how others might perceive them.

"Never, my lady." Sin hadn't paused to dwell on how his leaving Brownsea might affect his family, only what they all would gain from him going. Patience hadn't let the negative impact among society stop her crusade to educate others on the harmful consequences of pugilism. In this, they were much alike. "My hired hack is at your disposal."

Sin bowed and gestured toward his waiting conveyance.

With a mischievous grin, Patience nodded in return before slipping her hand into the crook of his elbow.

"Let us be off," she announced, her inflection matching that of her father's the day he'd rescued Sin from the alley close to Covent Gardens.

Sin could not help but note the rough, unpadded seat and filth that clung to the open hack as he took his seat across from Patience. This was not the mode of transportation the daughter of an earl should be relegated to. She deserved to move around town in an exquisitely adorned landau with velvet benches, a pan of hot coals at her feet, and brocade drapes covering the glass windowpanes. A finely attired driver at the reins with a competent footman near the boot should escort her to and fro her many societal entertainments.

"Where ta, m'lord?" the hack driver called, turning a toothy grin in their direction.

Sin swallowed the inadequacy that threatened to halt him before they'd even departed Southlund's House.

"Lyceum in the Strand, sir," Patience instructed.

"The Strand?" The driver focused on Sin, his brows raised high in question.

Sin looked between Patience and his driver.

"There is an empty lot, next to Daniel Mendoza's old academy." She twisted in her seat to face the man. "Do you know the place?"

"I do, m'lady, but—"

"Wonderful." Patience turned back to Sin, her smile returning as she settled her satchel on the seat next to her and folded her hands in her lap.

Sin nodded to the driver, and the hack pulled away from the walk and headed toward the Strand.

"May I ask after our destination?" Sin reclined in his seat, mirroring Patience's relaxed posture, careful not to show his unease.

The breeze created by the moving coach played with Patience's hair, pulling a few strands loose to brush across her face. Sin longed to reach forward and tuck the wayward locks behind her ear. Instead, he glanced over her shoulder as he waited for her to answer his question. He needed to remember that she'd agreed to train him and that was all. After his upcoming fight in Seven Dials, their association would come to an end. If not because his training would be complete, then because Patience would learn that he had no intention of it being his last match.

His need to not disappoint Lady Patience only went so far. Sin's goal when coming to London was to save his people.

"Daniel Mendoza"—she paused, her eyes widening—"you have heard of him, correct?"

"Of course," Sin grunted.

"Well, not long after my mother opened Southlund's House, Mendoza followed suit and organized a pugilist academy of his own. He was beyond his prime at that time and used his winnings to secure the building; however, in short order, the venture became too much, and his funds ran out. The academy closed, yet the boxers continued to gather." She brushed a strand of hair from her face before continuing. "It came to me last night, while I was assembling a new pamphlet, that your education is lacking. How many boxing matches have you witnessed?"

"Every day at Brownsea—"

"No," she cut in, shaking her head. "I mean true pugilist matches, not reckless amateurs who think the sport an admiral pastime. How many times have you stood and watched a real prizefight, taking note of movements and strategy as two accomplished boxers faced off? Much like you did on that first day at Southlund's, but a real match where opponents not only have wagers on the line but also their reputation."

Sin didn't need to ponder her question. He'd attended one match since his arrival in London—and the other two he'd been a part of: the skirmish in the alley, and his lost match at Bedford Square.

"You see, my lord, when a man is fighting for more than the prize purse of the match and survival and distinction is on the line, a base instinct is lit within the fighter that is absent during training. If you are to win your upcoming match, you must find that inner force and fire."

"You are wise beyond your years, Lady Patience," Sin replied. There was much more, beyond pugilism he could learn from the woman before him, and he couldn't help but long to know all the wisdom she had yet to share with him.

"No, I have seen too many boxers enter a match and risk their lives and well-being without the necessary skills." Her eyes met his across the open hack for the briefest of moments before she averted her stare. Sin suspected their conversation had brought to mind her mother.

For that, Sin held much regret.

Patience cleared her throat. "Let us pray that the rain holds off for at least an hour's time."

THEY STOOD, SHOULDER-TO-SHOULDER—or at least, side by side—on the fringe of what was commonly known as Mendoza's Yard, a cleared, empty lot with a level, hard-packed dirt surface where boxers of every skill level gathered to prove their worth. These fights were not about money or fame, but about showing skill on an even playing field. Pugilists chose their own matches with no wagers allowed. Day in and day out, as long as light gave them the ability to see, and the rain held off, men—and a few women—faced off against opponents of equal or greater skill. Fame and notoriety did not come from these matches; however, the potential of being discovered by men like Lord Holstrom was a possibility.

"This is not the hidden areas of Hyde Park or the back room of Gentleman Jackson's, my lady," Sin whispered close to her ear. Patience ignored the shiver that coursed through her, demanding that she not dwell on the reason behind it. Whether it was from their scandalous journey to the Strand or having Sin so close now, she did not have time to ponder.

"We are not in Mayfair any longer," Patience responded, sending a smirk in his direction. Not that she thought Sin wasn't accustomed to the seedier areas of London; however, the fighters who attended Mendoza's Yard were not the gentlemen who could afford the fees to train at Southlund's or the other notable pugilism clubs in town. "Do make me aware if anything offends your delicate sensibilities."

The jab was meant as a jest.

The earl was puzzling indeed.

He'd worked hard for days, left Southlund's battered and exhausted, yet he never complained as he adhered to her edicts. He listened, he learned, and he improved with each day. As the hours passed, their connection also evolved and developed, changing from two people thrown together by unfortunate circumstances to a relationship far more easy, natural…and confusing.

Yet, something… innate was lacking between them. He fought, and he fought hard, no longer relying on his brute prowess but tapping into his mental strength and cunning.

Self-preservation.

That was what was missing.

No matter the outcome of St. Seville's upcoming match in Seven Dials—win or lose—he would not be gravely affected beyond his debt to Holstrom. He had the choice to return to Brownsea Island, his home, to find another way to secure his lands and people. Many who fought did not have that option.

If they lost, they would not eat.

If they lost, they would have no bed, no fire, and no way of finding shelter from the harsh London winter.

If they lost, so did their families.

It was the way it was for Patience's mother, Ivory Bess, in her youth.

She had no country estate to retire to, no family or husband to see her through to the next match, and no one to count on but herself.

Even if the earl were never in such a dire situation, perhaps watching those who were, would give him the… Patience stumbled over the thought in her mind. Maybe it would give him the *heart* to win.

For all her mother's determination, skill, and love of the sport during her pugilist years, it had been heart that saw her through it all.

"This way, my lord." Patience walked forward to the edge of the yard as a pair of women, both attired in men's breeches and nothing but shifts to cover their bosoms, stepped to the line. She did not bother to glance at the earl to view his reaction. To some, it would look a spectacle. Though it was common in the world of boxing for women, same as their male counterparts, to strip bare to the waist. "That is Constance Country and Edith Woolgrower."

She felt his stare on her as she watched the women raise their fists.

"For a lady who claims to despise the sport, you know an awful lot about it."

"It was my mother's passion. I grew up with the sport surrounding me," she sighed. "I have not always found pugilism so distasteful. Miss Country and Miss Woolgrower were pupils of my mother's. We keep in contact, if only for me to continue my attempts to convince them both to seek other means of supporting themselves."

He clasped his hands behind his back and rocked onto the balls of his feet. "I see."

The softness in his tone told Patience that he did, in fact, see and understand.

For the next hour, Patience stood close to St. Seville, his tall, broad stature blocking the wind from her face as they watched match after match. Men, women, and even a set of youngsters no older than thirteen took to the yard to prove their worth, show their skill, and pray—most fruitlessly—to be recognized and whisked away from the poverty and desperation of their current lives.

If Patience had the resources to rescue them all, she would…without a second thought.

Yet, for every five she helped, another hundred would go without. And even those she helped sometimes found their way back to this cold, harsh life.

The earl didn't question her about why they ventured to the Strand, nor did he talk endlessly as they watched the fighters.

Eventually, a warmth settled at her back, and she was startled to find his hand pressed firmly there in an almost possessive way.

A measure of comfort and safety settled around her, though Patience hadn't needed it. Not many years ago, this had been Patience's world. Not the startling poverty of the fighters, but the world of bare-knuckle boxing. She didn't need a man at her side to reassure or protect her.

She was happy for it now, all the same.

Many in London society never witnessed this side of town life. The less fortunate were relegated to their boroughs, and the nobles preferred to act as if they didn't exist as they shielded themselves from the reality of London with their drawn drapes in their fine carriages as they traveled through areas rife with hardship.

It was the same with prizefighters. Those who had demonstrated their skills and had been picked from obscurity and chosen to compete in elite matches all over London tried to forget the men and women who attended places like Mendoza's Yard. Eventually, those great fighters fell, and another crop was plucked from places like the Strand and thrust into the light for a brief moment of fame and notoriety.

Patience shook her head in sorrow as her stomach twisted into a knot. Perhaps it had been a mistake to bring St. Seville here. He'd been born into privilege, the son of a nobleman secure in his future. The importance of places like Mendoza's Yard couldn't have meaning and impact for a lord of St. Seville's station.

Still, his hand lay solidly on her back, her shoulder brushing his side.

When had she tucked herself into him?

St. Seville was not the one to offer her security or even comfort. He was her pupil, and there could be nothing more between them despite the closeness that had matured between them. It was the way of things after so many hours of training. Boxers developed innate connections to those who taught them, and trainers became burdened with the need to see their pupil successfully through their matches.

A single warm droplet of rain landed on her cheek. Patience wiped it away and turned to see the menacing clouds gathering above. The storm was nearly upon them. If they did not return to Southlund's House with haste, they would be caught in the downpour.

Stepping away, Patience glanced behind them to the hack the earl had bid wait for them. "I think it is time we go."

No one took notice of them as they departed the yard. St. Seville's height and formidable width drew little attention in an area such as this. Nor did Patience's simple skirt and blouse draw undue fascination from the crowd.

Climbing aboard the hack, St. Seville took the seat next to her.

"My lord?" she asked, as if being alone with the earl, unchaperoned in the Strand, was not enough to cause a scandal, but sitting side by side would push them into dangerous territory.

A smattering of raindrops covered his face when he looked down at her. "The rain will only increase on our drive. The least I can do, after everything you've taught me, is keep you from catching your death of cold."

To prove his point, he slipped from his coat and wrapped it around her shoulders and head to block the rain from drenching her as they started toward Southlund's House.

Patience nestled closer to St. Seville, allowing his warmth and the scent of him to wash over her as the rain would have if he hadn't created a makeshift shelter for her.

It was such a simple gesture, yet one she was wholly unfamiliar with. Not because her father and brothers didn't attempt to shield her. Mainly because she never allowed anyone this close, finding fault with every man who sought her hand.

Shifting, Patience looked up at the earl. Surprisingly, his stare was focused on her, as well—but not on her eyes. No, his narrowed, russet-brown eyes were trained on her lips.

Heat coursed through her, banishing the frigid cold that stung her reddened nose and seeped through her gloves.

Patience had never been faced with such a situation.

The earl leaned closer, and her lips parted as her tongue darted across her bottom lip. Something in her chest fluttered at the same time she exhaled. She fisted her hands in her lap to keep from reaching out for him, laying her gloved palm on his cheek and drawing his face to hers.

Suddenly, the hack dipped and jostled, hitting an uneven patch in the street and tossing Patience back a few inches. Not far, but enough to break whatever spell had kept the earl's focus trained on her lips. His jacket slipped down to the seat behind her.

Rain sprinkled her face, and Patience laughed.

The sound seemed foreign and strained, even to her own ears.

The earl coughed and straightened, retrieving his jacket and lifting it up once again to cover her, but he did not lean close again. Instead, he retreated to the far corner of the hack.

Patience searched her brain for something—anything—to draw him close again.

The moment had faded…gone as swiftly as it had set upon them.

"I shall collect you tomorrow evening at the Albany, and we will set out for Seven Dials?" Patience still needed to figure out how to dissuade Merit and Valor from tagging along on her escapade to West End. And now, it seemed all the more important to keep the earl hidden. They had tomorrow evening, and then Patience's obligation to St. Seville would come to an end.

Win or lose, the earl had agreed that this would be his final prizefight.

What would come then? Could she return to her crusade against pugilism? Draft more pamphlets and send her father into hazardous boroughs to distribute them as if she hadn't been training a fighter only a few nights before? Could she be content to return to the life she'd led up until the night she stumbled upon the earl bare-chested and escaping her house?

She sighed, but the sound was swallowed up by the wind as the rain increased.

CHAPTER 13

SIN PUSHED HIS untouched meal around on his plate, his appetite stalled by the note from Lady Patience—and the prizefight starting in two hours' time. *I will meet you in Seven Dials.* How was he supposed to interpret that? Her missive only held those seven simple words. She hadn't signed her name or written her message on monogrammed stationery. If anyone had intercepted it, there would be nothing that could be traced back to its sender. Even the young boy who'd knocked on his door at the Albany had been paid two pence to make certain Patience's note went to no one but the *bloke with hair like a seaman.*

They'd trained—hard—the day before, and then had gone to the Strand. Before they parted ways, she'd instructed him that she would arrive at the Albany to collect him. Had something occurred? Had their moment in the hack frightened her? For most of the night, Sin had thought it perhaps only he who'd felt the connection between them. The draw was undeniable, no matter how Sin attempted to ignore it.

Maybe Desmond had discovered her absences from Marsh Manor each day when she journeyed to

Southlund's House to work with Sin and forbade her to leave the house?

Their hours together had quickly turned from exhaustive physical exertion to fleeting minutes where Sin longed for them to stretch on and on. With her tutelage, his movements had become more precise, and his agility increased with each session. Patience's skill in the ring only shone more with each hour as men attended the club to watch the daughter of the famed pugilist, Ivory Bess.

If there were anything more than just her offer to train him connecting them, Sin would have been jealous of every fighter who stood gaping around the ring as they worked. Sin had no claims to Lady Patience—not on her attention or her affection.

"Yes, the man claimed to be a gentleman, though we all know Blankenship's less than proper tendencies," the man across from Sin said with a chuckle. "Come now, toes! Have you heard any such vile thing?"

Sin chuckled along with the trio who'd invited him to dine with them before they all made their way to Seven Dials.

Coventry was set on introducing Sin to as many of his wicked men as possible, as if that would keep him in London once he earned the funds needed to return home to Brownsea.

The Earl of Harrington and Davenport were friendly enough. Quite a bit younger than Coventry, but close to Sin's age, the pair each sported the unmistakable mark of Coventry's club—the golden *W* pinned to their lapel.

Sin had left his in his room at the Albany, and he'd noted Coventry's disapproval when he first entered the Wicked Earls' Club.

Besides the matching pins, the men favored similar hairstyles trimmed above their collars with tresses that flopped long in the front. They were not men Sin would find any sort of connection with had he been on his home isle, but in London, they seemed to be the usual proper, dapper lords about town.

Their conversation varied between jesting about a certain lord to talk of coming balls and even ventured so far as to delve into bets they'd made recently at White's.

Sin held his breath, willing his headache to subside.

Coventry remained silent for most of the meal, as had Sin, allowing Harrington and Davenport to drone on and on about *ton* gossip—mainly referring to lords and ladies Sin had never heard of.

"Did you hear about ol' Pembroke?" Harrington took a long sip from his ale as he glanced around the table. When no one offered any response, he continued, "He's found himself a bride. Rumor has it she is as beautiful as the night and equally as mysterious. A high-born lady who could do far better than the likes of Pembroke."

"I heard they're already wed…out of necessity, if you know what I mean," Davenport countered, bringing his hands up as if he held an extended belly.

If Sin had missed the meaning of his words, he would have understood the gesture well. This Pembroke fellow had gotten a woman with child, certainly not the worst occurrence, especially if the man were smitten with the lady in question.

"The lot of you would do well to secure a match with a fine woman—start a family before you're too old and grey to attract anything but the lightskirts who fancy Vauxhall." Coventry signaled the servant for another drink. "I have met the Countess of Pembroke, and she is a lovely, beautiful, wise young lady."

Sin half listened as the conversation continued, but Coventry's warning and Harrington's jest about this man Pembroke had Sin's thoughts returning to Lady Patience. The daughter of an earl—a lord who happened to be one of his father's friends. Her dark countenance and single-minded determination were much akin to his own. Yet, similar to Pembroke and his lady fair, Patience deserved a life far above that which Sin lived: tilling the soil, mending his tenants' roofs, taking his land's crops to market in Dorset. That was what kept Sin occupied.

Lady Patience deserved a gentleman who would lavish her with beautiful, handmade gowns and shining gems. A lord who knew his way around society with friends of great prestige. A learned man.

Not a male of oxen portions who would fare better at sea than in a London ballroom.

Despite all her words and actions to the contrary, she appeared resolute in her place outside the norms of society. But Sin could not believe that was what she wanted for the rest of her life.

Why had the thought even come to mind? Patience was assisting him in the art of pugilism, nothing more. They had no other attachments beyond the sport. Soon enough, he would have the funds he needed to return home, and she would remain in London. Time—and distance—would erase their memories of one another. Their association would likely end long before Sin returned to Brownsea Island.

"Do you know anything about Devin Parsons?" Coventry broke into Sin's depressing thoughts.

"Parsons?" Sin asked, glancing up to see all three men staring at him. "Should I know the man?"

Harrington chuckled, turning a huge grin at Davenport. "I told you we made the correct wager."

Sin was growing exhausted with the back and forth between the gentlemen, and his headache increased. Why had he agreed to accompany Coventry for dinner in the first place? Because he'd been wallowing for hours after receiving Patience's note that she'd meet him at the fight as opposed to them making the trip together.

It shouldn't upset him. He hadn't wanted her to attend the fight at all.

"What wager?" Coventry inquired.

"We placed a bet at White's last evening when word of the match circulated." Harrington turned a hesitant glance in Sin's direction. "We know St. Seville is a formidable lord; nonetheless, Parsons has trained with the likes of John Gully and was declared the victor against Tom Cribb some years back."

Davenport straightened in his chair, his head swinging back and forth between Sin and Coventry. "I told him that meant nothing. Just because Parsons seems the obvious pick, doesn't mean St. Seville here can't knock him down a peg or two. However, because I lost to Harrington in regards to the Duke of Mulberry's situation, I had to allow him his way."

Sin could only imagine what the Duke of Mulberry's situation entailed.

"You scoundrels," Coventry shouted with a booming laugh, bringing the attention of the entire room to them. "You wagered *against* St. Seville?"

"Not my choice," Davenport shrugged. "The Duke of Mulberry's situation, remember?"

"Quiet down," Sin hissed, leaning forward. "Does everyone think I am to lose?"

The Wicked Earls' Club was brimming with men—eating, drinking, gambling, and playing billiards before setting off on their evening's entertainments. When he'd entered, Sin had overheard a group of gentlemen discussing their plans to attend the opera that night and how they could extricate themselves and accompany Coventry to Seven Dials for the prizefight instead.

While Sin hadn't necessarily settled in among the group of earls, he also hadn't gotten the sense that he wouldn't be accepted if it were something he wanted. But now…

"Thirty to one odds, I'm afraid," Harrington said.

"Based on the outcome of your fight in Bedford Square, I'd say that some misguided fools have faith in your ability that I do not. Doesn't mean I don't believe you to be a fine chap, but money is money, and you know my dear grandfather, the old fool, thinks if he starves my allowance, I will return to the fold."

"He does have his sights set on bringing you to heel at any cost, does he not?" Davenport winked at Harrington.

"The Devil of Davenport thinks to make a jest about my financial situation?" Harrington leveled back.

Sin couldn't help but wonder if the men were friends or enemies. It was hard to tell with their back and forth bickering.

"Time to go, gentlemen." Coventry dabbed at the corners of his mouth before laying the cloth on his empty plate. "If Sin is tardy, he will certainly have little chance of besting Parsons."

"Better than no chance, I suppose," Davenport said, following Coventry from his seat. "Has anyone seen Grayson of late?"

Sin trailed Coventry away from the table, uninterested in Harrington's answer. Another man Sin had never heard of nor cared about; though no doubt a lord with problems as grand as Sin's troubles. Was that what connected all these men more securely than their station as earls?

He tapped his foot in anticipation as they waited for their jackets. Never would Lady Patience bore him with talk of people he was unfamiliar with. They had trained for nearly five hours the previous day, and not once had they broached a subject not to Sin's liking. Every moment, he was enthralled with either her words or the way her trim body executed moves his larger frame could not manage.

Neither did she deem his financial problems as anything unsolvable.

Lady Patience Lane had faith in him, Sinclair Chambers, the Earl of St. Seville.

Perhaps more faith than anyone he'd yet to meet. Even his mother had been leery of his decision to travel to London. But this woman did more than just believe in him, she gave him a new sense of hope—or at least, the belief that it was possible to rectify his problems.

"Let us be off." Coventry clapped Sin on the back, startling him. "Do not mind Harrington and Davenport, they run the odds in every wager. Pays off most days. But this time, I suspect they shall suffer a loss."

"That would make two people who have faith in my abilities," Sin mumbled.

"I do hope we aren't made to look the fool." Coventry started for the door, and Sin realized the earl thought Sin had been talking about himself.

Sin might be an utter fool; however, Lady Patience had proven herself to be anything but.

CHAPTER 14

LADY PATIENCE HELD a rose-scented kerchief to her nose as they rode deeper and deeper into the West End past Covent Gardens, the aromas of the muck-filled streets invading the carriage. The sun had set several hours before, and the deserted pathways were only infrequently invaded by a lone figure on foot or horseback. How the men and women here survived in such a harrowing, violent area, Patience was uncertain.

Thankfully, the match had been set up in Seven Dials as opposed to St. Giles, where rumors circulated that gang violence had increased tenfold since autumn. It made little sense to Patience that a mere handful of blocks could make such a difference. What made territory in St. Giles worth clashing over, while Seven Dials was left miserable and contemptible? The rookeries—Whitechapel, St. Giles, and Seven Dials—were not places for any respectable woman; however, Patience would not forsake Sin.

She pulled the drape back a mere inch to peek out at the hazy, dark night to see few lights burning in the windows as they traveled down a pothole-ridden dirt alley. The hardships of the people who sought the rookeries as their home was no secret to Patience. They were her countrymen, though they hailed from many parts of the world. A plan formulated as she allowed the drape to fall back into place. Perhaps her pamphlets would be better received and understood if there were more illustrations to help those who were not adequately educated. How had she not thought of this before now?

"Are you certain we are going in the correct direction?" Merit shifted on the bench next to her. "The smell is horrendous, and my back is aching from the jostling."

"I did not force you to accompany me," Patience retorted.

Valor extended his legs into Patience's sparse space and crossed his ankles. "I hadn't any plans for this evening anyways, though I would be put in a dour mood, indeed, if I were to be pinched while in such an unsavory area."

"Father would replace your coins," Merit chuckled. "Though he could not restore your mettle."

"What is that supposed to mean?" Valor kicked at Merit, blessedly giving Patience room for her half boots once again.

Oftentimes, Patience was hard-pressed to believe that Valor was the eldest sibling, especially when he allowed Merit to tease him to anger so easily.

"Do be quiet." Patience rubbed her temples. "The pair of you is giving me a headache. I am as anxious as you to arrive, for then I will have the freedom to be away from you two."

"And I thought Merit most resembled Father." It was Valor's turn to prod Merit to irritation.

"I can see why you returned to London so quickly." Patience dropped her hands back to her lap, knowing that no amount of massaging would relieve the tension in her head. It wasn't only her brothers' bickering that caused the ache, but the thought of Sin facing another opponent when he wasn't ready. A handful of lessons was not enough to learn what took years to master. Even she had dedicated years to gaining the skill she possessed, and many fighters spent decades training. How could Sin compare after only a few days? Part of her feared she was sending him into a losing battle. "You likely went on like schoolboys at the country party, and the host ended the gathering early just to be away from the pair of you."

Merit stiffened next to her even though he shook his head at her words.

"Where, exactly, are we going?" Valor pulled a flat, tall bottle from his inside jacket pocket, twisted off the cap, and took a long sip before handing it across the space to Merit. "You have been awfully secretive about all of this."

Patience ignored his question and grabbed for the bottle, snatching it before Merit could. Bringing it to her nose, she sniffed, immediately regretting her decision. The vile odor of spirits invaded her senses, bringing a sudden and punishing sting to her nose.

"Is this"—She took another much smaller sniff of the bottle—"gin?"

Valor sat up straight, his shoulders thrown back. "It is none of your concern what we, proper gentlemen of the *ton*, take as our libation."

"Besides, Father won't miss one bottle of gin," Merit said, his words more hopeful than his tone. "If we decide to partake in spirits, it is our business."

Patience stoppered the bottle and slipped it between her hip and the side of the coach. Perhaps her father sheltered them all a bit too much. Valor, at twenty-five, should be concerned with wooing a wife, preparing for his place in Parliament, and securing the necessary associations in society to see himself a formidable lord—when the day came he inherited the

Desmond earldom. And Merit, though four years Valor's junior, should be making his way in London and finding a path for his future as the second son. Perhaps a commission in the Navy or investment in profitable merchant ventures to the New World.

Instead, they were more concerned with attending extravagant country parties, gambling, and drinking. At least neither had taken up with a wedded woman or courtesan, Patience reminded herself.

Merit huffed, and Valor trained his narrowed stare on her, most likely thinking to intimidate her into returning the bottle.

"Our destination is a building on Queen Street in Seven Dials," Patience said, satisfied to see both men lose their dour expressions. "Having our wits about us is important. The match will be attended by many wealthy, titled men, but also by the thieves, panderers, and debauched drunkards who call Seven Dials home."

Both men turned to gaze out their side windows and, not for the first time, she wondered how they could possibly be siblings. Patience had taken on her mother's, and father's, tendency for helping those less fortunate than them. Her brothers had embraced their station as the sons of the Earl of Desmond. There was little doubt that Valor, once he inherited the title, would join Coventry's coven of misfit earls.

With Merit in tow, they would spend their time drinking and gambling away the fortune their father had amassed for them.

Perhaps it would be wise for Patience to find a husband, wed, and collect her dowry before her brothers found a way to flit it away. Her father would not be so naive as to not safeguard her portion of the money left to her by her mother—and what was settled upon her by the earldom.

Marriage.

Patience snorted at the notion.

Had times turned so desperate that she actually considered taking a man to husband as a necessary means to secure her future? The idea hadn't crossed her mind, let alone taken root and become in any way appealing to her, since before her mother died—back when her future had been bright. Before the clouds of sorrow and loss had obliterated any picture of what her future could hold.

With the loss of her mother came the stark knowledge that her future would not be that of what little girls dreamed of.

Her sisters, Verity and Temperance, were the proper ladies who took after the Desmond side of their lineage, while Patience had always aligned with her mother's family. Not that she—or any of her siblings—had ever met their mother's kin; however, her sisters' tendencies to go about town spending obscene amounts of coin and dressing in gowns that cost more than the sum of an entire boarding house in Seven Dials seemed misguided and foolish to Patience.

And here they were, returning to the borough Ivory Bess had called home until her twentieth birthday. Odd, that it was the same age Patience currently was. She could not so much as fathom the squalor her mother had endured until she was rescued by the young, dashing Earl of Desmond. It was the reason her father stored gin as opposed to brandy or scotch. It had been his wife's favorite.

Perhaps that had been why Patience insisted on attending the prizefight with Sin. Not because she feared for him but because she searched for a connection to her mother that did not revolve around pain and sorrow.

Her motive was certainly not solely the Earl of St. Seville—a man as devilishly handsome as his moniker.

Win or lose, he would return home soon enough, and their brief association would be forgotten.

Though she did fervently long for him to best his opponent, even if that meant he collected the prize and held to his promise not to fight again—and his imminent departure from London. This was exactly what she wanted, so why was it unappealing now?

The carriage dipped suddenly, knocking Patience off balance and into Merit before their driver pulled the horses to a stop and set the brake.

Her trepidation at the coming fight coursed through her once again. The entertainment her brothers offered had been welcome while it lasted, but now, they'd arrived. There was no way to distract her from the coming match.

"We have arrived, my lady," her driver called. The conveyance shifted, and the door swung open, followed by her footman setting down the steps. Due to the location of the prizefight, Patience had insisted that a footman accompany their driver. "We shall wait here for your return."

As Patience collected her handbag, Merit and Valor departed the carriage, neither waiting to assist her down. She swallowed to keep her irritation at bay as she took the driver's hand and stepped to the walk—nothing but a dirt walkway alongside the dilapidated, windowless building. Against the decaying wood at the bottom of the building were piles of rotten waste and what appeared to be a forgotten wool blanket.

Glancing up and down the street, Patience noticed an open door with light pooling out onto the street beyond as two men, collars raised and hands deep in their pockets slipped inside.

"This way," she bid her two brothers, once again taking the lead. As they neared the open door, loud voices floated out on the cool night breeze: laughter, carousing, and conversation. Not unlike many of the prizefights she'd accompanied her mother to in the past. Thankfully, her blood didn't freeze in her veins upon entering the building as it had when she arrived at the match in Bedford Square. The building was teeming with men and women from all classes, some dressed as fine London dandies, others garbed in merchant attire, and women with gowns so scanty that their bosoms threatened to fall from their tight bodices.

There was nothing like war and prizefights to bring together every class of Englishmen and women.

Patience turned to lecture her brothers about the importance of…

But they were already gone, weaving their way through the mingling crowd. Likely headed toward the makeshift bar in the corner of the room to procure themselves drinks.

In a heartbeat, they'd disappeared from view.

Patience lowered her head and pushed into the crowd when she noted two men, their eyes locked on her, moving quickly in her direction. Did they think her a woman of ill repute—a lady who preferred the entertainments of the night?

There was no blaming them, Patience mused as her eyes darted from one scandalously clad woman to the next. It was not only the prizefighters and wager takers who were working this night. Her heart ached for the women who'd been forced to find their way in life by selling their bodies.

That could have been her own mother's fate had she not met the Earl of Desmond. There were limited means for survival for women who'd grown too old to fight—or lacked the expertise to train others.

Patience scanned the crowd as she pushed her way toward the fighting area in the middle of the large, open warehouse, though it was made difficult by her slight height. There were several men she recognized from around London—the young, handsome Duke of Chastain, the aging father of Lady Haversham, as well as Lord and Lady Maddox.

How had Holstrom managed to gather so many of London's upper crust in such a dubious location?

Still, she did not see Sin or Lord Holstrom as she reached the edge of the pugilist area. For a brief moment, she feared Sin hadn't received her note and still awaited her arrival at the Albany, but a feverish applause rang out as the entire room erupted in cheers. From the far side of the room, the fighters, Sin and Parsons, entered the warehouse, both already stripped to the waist. Holstrom was not looking to bolster wagers—there would be no delaying the prizefight while men scrambled about the room cataloging and collecting coins.

If she had to guess, Holstrom and his ilk had been collecting wagers in far more wealthy locales. Bets had been placed long before the *beau monde* departed their fine London townhomes and elegantly adorned clubs, for the seedy, licentious West End.

Patience gave a quick wave to Sin as he strode toward the gathered crowd, pushing and shoving to gain a better view of the match to come, but his narrowed, pensive glare never landed on her—or anything, as much as she could tell. His mouth remained pressed into a firm line as he ignored the comments from his opponent. Sin stood close to Parsons, and his shoulders were equally as broad, as their shadows, cast from the light behind the fighters, stretched all the way to the toe of Patience's half boots. His hair was tied back securely with a length of twine, and the stubble that had dusted his face the day before had doubled in length overnight.

Sin appeared fierce…the dark circles under his eyes only adding to his intimidating nature. Even his busted lip made him look rugged and brutal, though he'd gotten the injury at a fight he'd lost.

The clamor of hushed whispers behind her said the crowd was having the same reaction to Sin as she.

In a striking correlation, Parsons stood at Sin's left,

taller than Sin with muscles straining at taut skin. Two Corinthians facing off in a bare-knuckle match was certain to lessen the impact of all she'd taught Sin.

Muscle and sheer size would mean nothing in this ring as they each possessed an overabundance of both. A fighter worth their weight in gold needed cunning and agility.

Despite his opponent's size, confidence radiated from Sin—the same unbridled brashness that had led to him lose against Povolti.

While she was infused with an alarming amount of dread.

Yet, Parsons stood with similar self-assurance as Lord Holstrom strode into the open area and raised his arms, signaling for silence.

"Gentlemen, ladies…and"—Holstrom paused, holding his hand to his forehead as if blocking out the bright rays of the sun—"my good countrymen!"

It was all the crowd needed to break into another round of cheers and jeers.

Patience spotted her brothers, ale tankards in hands, howling from about twenty paces to her left. They'd also pushed their way to the front of the gathering. Did they not have the same sick feeling rolling through their stomachs at the very thought of the upcoming match?

Valor and Merit were older than she…they'd had more years with their mother, and yet they'd so seamlessly—almost effortlessly—moved past her loss.

Everything within Patience was in turmoil. Her stomach tightened at the same time the hairs on the back of her neck stood on end with excitement. Her palms grew clammy at the same time her heart pounded with anticipation. Excitement and anticipation. The two overwhelming sensations that'd coursed through her when she and her mother had waited at the side of the ring as the pugilists took their places and prepared for the match—just as Sin and Parsons did now.

Sin, all toned, defined muscle.

Parsons, boiling with unspent endurance.

During her years in the schoolroom, Patience had snuck from her studies to watch the fighters, marveling at their discipline.

In that moment, she could only think of the repercussions when their time in the ring ended. Everything was on the line for Sin. Losing would mean he was further indebted to Holstrom. Winning would mean… What would it mean beyond proving that Patience's short training sessions had helped and that Sin could make his way as a pugilist?

Holstrom made a show of announcing the featured fighters and listing the rules of the match…the Broughton Rules. They were the same guidelines all prizefights had followed for nearly eighty years, another fact she'd learned during her time at Southlund's House. The fight would continue for as many rounds as necessary until one of the fighters was unable to stand or return to the scratch line. Thirty seconds of rest between rounds. Each round would end when one of the fighters went down or took a knee.

There was no limit to the number of rounds to be fought, and the match could last for hours. It was endurance Patience feared Sin lacked.

Though his strength—paired with the defensive maneuvers she'd taught him—would hopefully see the prizefight ended before the midnight church bells tolled. If the men were lucky, they'd both leave Seven Dials with only superficial wounds to their faces, bruises on their torsos, and aching hands.

Worst case, Patience would need her brothers' help to get Sin to her carriage—his face a bloodied mess or his hands broken.

She refused to think of any graver injury befalling Sin. It was not an uncommon occurrence for fighters to severely injure their fists. Perhaps it was far more widespread than the undetectable damage done to a boxer's mind from the impact of continual blows to the head.

Patience closed her eyes and took a deep, labored inhale, holding the air in her lungs until they burned. He'd promised one more fight…to gain his freedom from Holstrom. Then she'd never have to worry about her mother's fate becoming Sin's. She could see this through and be there for him after it was over. She understood his desperate need to help his family. She could only imagine the great lengths she'd go to if one of her siblings or her father were in peril.

Perhaps it would be best for her to slip from the warehouse and await the end of the match in her carriage. There was no doubt she could—and would—handle the aftermath of the prizefight. She was adequate at caring for injured pugilists. There was a mindset that propelled her, as it had her mother, during those moments after a match ended.

Now would be no different…win or lose.

Or perhaps it was different…entirely, completely, utterly different.

Because it was Sin standing in the ring. It was Sin preparing to fight against a pugilist of high caliber. There was more at risk than mere money and reputation.

A spectator jostled Patience from behind, and her eyes sprang up to see Sin take a jab to the face. Her chest seized. His nose and lip took the brunt of the impact. Her heart soared when Parsons' next volley of fists connected with air as Sin sidestepped and ducked, pivoting swiftly to throw a punch into his opponent's side, right below his ribcage.

Parsons' strangled groan echoed in the building as he fell forward to the dirt floor, ending the round.

The crowd cheered and chanted, "Sin, Sin, Sin!"

Sin moved to the far corner of the clearing, his chest shining with sweat, and his lip bleeding, but other than that, he appeared well. Parsons pushed to his feet and moved to the opposite side, breathing heavily as his arms snaked around his midsection.

She couldn't bring herself to shout for either fighter.

The brutal sport, no matter how much her mother had adored it, was—at its core—violent and destructive.

Though that did not stop Valor and Merit from clasping Sin on the back where he waited out the half minute until he made his way back to the scratch line for the next round.

Her hands clenched before her until her fingers ached from the tension.

This wasn't right. Patience wasn't supposed to be here. A man she cared for shouldn't have taken to the ring. And despite all her attempts to fool herself into thinking she only had a stake in his fighting ability, Patience bloody well cared for the lord—more than she'd ever dreamed possible. It wasn't her need to spread news of the dangers of pugilism that had made her propose her condition he never fight again; it was because she desperately, madly, insanely cared for him. She wanted no harm to come to him, no matter the cause.

At that thought, Sin glanced in her direction and nodded. His grin was wide as he brushed a strand of hair from his eyes.

Her heart shuddered as he raised his bare fists and continued to stare at her.

Every eye in the warehouse turned to see who had captured the prizefighter's attention, even Valor and Merit.

Patience should have fled the match when she had the chance; instead, she was helpless to do anything but watch as Sin moved to the scratch line, and her brothers

176 | *Christina McKnight*

pushed their way toward her, their identical confused expressions trained on Patience.

While she only had eyes—and heart—for Sin.

CHAPTER 15

ROUND AFTER ROUND continued until they blurred together into one long string of thrown fists. Sin bested his opponent in more rounds than he—or Holstrom—had anticipated. The chilly air in the room was kept at bay by the layer of sweat that clung to his exposed skin. His core remained hot from his physical exertion, though the cold breeze from the open doors stung his busted lip. The skin on his knuckles had cracked open several rounds ago, and the ground between him and Parsons was covered in both fighters' blood.

Never had Sin fought so hard or for so long.

His fists screamed in pain, begged him to put an end to the fight.

But all Sin could picture was his family and his people—at Brownsea Island—who relied on him. He had to win his freedom from Holstrom, make a name for himself as a pugilist, and do his damnedest to earn enough coin to return home with his head held high, knowing his people would not starve, and his mother and sister would not go without even the barest of necessities.

A droplet of sweat slid down his forehead into his eye, causing his vision to blur as he blinked away the insufferable nuisance.

For not the first time, he glanced at the crowd to see Lady Patience—her eyes wide and her own hands balled into fists at her sides—as she watched him. Though the crowd was loud with their cheers and taunts, Patience was like a stone statue. She didn't champion either fighter nor did she even so much as move. How many rounds had he glimpsed her standing thusly? Five? Six? More?

Every part of Sin wished he didn't have to do the one thing that brought her anguish and disappointment.

And soon, she'd learn that he'd lied about his future intentions.

Holstrom called for the next round to commence, and Sin moved aggressively toward Parsons. It was time the match came to an end…and Sin had every intention of being deemed the victor. Povolti had bested him rather easily, only three rounds into their match, but Sin had learned much from his lessons with Patience. Enough, at least, to best his current opponent.

The opportunity presented itself a few minutes into the round.

Parsons swayed on his feet, and his fists dropped to his sides, giving Sin ample time to advance on the man before his defenses rose again.

It was either take his shot now or face more rounds. Sin had to beat Parsons to the punch. Literally.

Sin bobbed, weaved, and threw a corkscrew punch into his opponent's side, the exact place where his blow had landed in the first round. Parsons had appeared dazed for the last several rounds, and Sin wasn't brutal enough to send his winning punch to the man's head, especially with Patience's warnings about head injuries fresh in Sin's thoughts.

Retreating, Sin watched as Parsons stumbled

sideways before righting himself, only to careen the other direction and into the crowd.

Spectators halted Parsons and pushed him back into the ring.

As the crowd shouted at Parsons, he fell to the ground, his lids drooping closed.

Holstrom started his count, "One…two…three…"

Sin's defense crumbled, and his fists opened and fell to his sides as he sucked in large gulps of air. Blood trailed down his chin and dripped onto his chest.

Abject horror etched Patience's face as she turned, her body trembling. The reaction disappeared in the blink of an eye, and she rushed toward him at the same time the crowd let loose with their pent-up shouts, some in celebration of bets won and others of money lost.

It was only when she didn't stop before him but threw herself at his chest that Sin sprang into action, catching her as she landed against him and wrapped her arms around his neck.

Her heart beat against his chest, in time with his own, and her blue-grey eyes stared up to meet his.

He longed to reassure her that he was well and mostly unharmed, but the words stuck in his throat at the unexpected feel of her body pressed against his.

She trembled again, and Sin was helpless to keep his body under control as it shivered along with hers.

"Tell me you are well," she breathed, the scent of her evening meal lingering between them. "The blood, there is so much blood, I"—Her words cut off as a sob escaped—"I would never forgive myself if something grave happened to you."

"I am well enough." He brushed his fingers down her cheek but pulled his hand back quickly before his blood marred her exquisite, creamy skin. "I am whole, and it is over."

Sin promised silently that Patience would never be present to witness him fight again. It was too much, too excruciating to see her like this. His head spun when he thought about what she'd go through if he lost again. He could not put her through it.

He slowly lowered her to the ground, never removing his stare from hers.

But when her feet touched the hard-packed dirt, the connection between them broke, and the cheers from the spectators invaded their brief moment of privacy. People pushed forward to give Sin their congratulations and shake his hand or clap him on the back for a fight well won.

One man stepped directly in between him and Patience, bringing a growl from Sin. The offender gave a gruff hear-hear before beating a hasty retreat.

Next, it was Holstrom at his side, pulling at his elbow to dislodge Sin from the crush.

Patience smiled weakly and gestured for Sin to speak with Holstrom.

"I will wait for you outside," she said. "My carriage isn't far."

He could only nod because he knew bloody well what Patience expected him to do, what Sin had promised he'd do.

Turning to follow Holstrom, Sin could not allow Patience to witness his guilt.

She wouldn't hear the conversation between him and Holstrom.

As he followed the lord toward the area farthest from the crowd, they both paused to watch Parsons being assisted from the building and out the same door he and Sin had entered through. There was a physician waiting in the back room to see to both fighters if necessary, and Sin supposed Parsons would be taking advantage of the good doctor.

Perhaps it would be wise to have the man tend to Sin's cut knuckles and broken lip, as well.

"Well done, St. Seville," Coventry said when he,

Davenport, and Harrington joined Sin and Holstrom. "I told these two simpletons they were misguided in wagering against you."

"It isn't as if we do not have the funds to lose," Harrington mumbled. "But it is still crushing."

"Coventry," Holstrom chuckled the deep echo of a satisfied man. "I must say, your lord here had the heart of a true prizefighter."

"Did I not tell you in my letter? His first showing wasn't great; however, give him a good scolding, and some incentive, and look what he accomplishes."

Sin focused his attention on Coventry and Holstrom's feet as his temper flared. They spoke as if he were nothing but livestock taken to auction—whipped and taunted into performing as he should. What other option did Sin have?

Forego competing in any future matches, take his prize money, and return to Brownsea Island only to be in dire straits by the next winter? It was almost too much to bear, and would only serve to harm his family.

Holstrom held out a purse to Sin. "Your prize," he said, giving the velvet bag a shake when Sin didn't immediately snatch it from him. "Well earned. The next fight should provide a purse twice—or even thrice—this amount."

Sin, as well as Coventry and the other two lords, stared at the swinging bag. It might as well have been dripping with blood, as his hands were after the fight. He didn't want to collect his due, but it was the reason he'd fought in the first place. Yet, taking it, Sin knew he was agreeing to continue as Holstrom's pawn, fighting when he was summoned.

And in turn, he'd need to lie to Lady Patience, end their friendship, and never look back.

It was inconceivable to believe that Sin would be able to look the lady in the eye and outright deceive her.

Could he chance the future of his estate and his

family for Lady Patience Lane? A woman he'd known for such a short time?

Sin grabbed the bag before Holstrom drew it back and slipped it into the pocket of his trousers.

"When is the next match?" There was only his responsibility to his estate that could matter, that should matter—not Lady Patience or her anger if she learned of his continued fighting. Patience had a family who cared for her, while the St. Seville people only had Sin to depend on. He could not let them down. Not even if that meant securing Patience's happiness. "I will need a day or so to rest, but after that—"

"Do not worry, St. Seville," Holstrom chuckled, glancing past Sin. The crowd, though still loud, was likely thinning as the spectators moved out of the warehouse to continue their evening. "It will be a couple of days. I think you and I are going to earn quite the sum from our next prizefight."

"You plan to fight again?" It was a whisper at his back but thundered through Sin as if it were shouted directly in his face. "I thought you—*we* agreed…"

The last word ended on a sob, and Sin's chin dipped toward his chest.

He couldn't turn around, hadn't the courage to face her.

She wasn't supposed to hear, she wasn't supposed to know, she was supposed to await him at her carriage.

Sin had made the mistake of not keeping watch over her until she'd left the building.

Bloody hell, he should have walked her to the carriage and returned only after he made certain she was safely inside.

"Perhaps you live up to your name in more ways than one, *my lord*," she seethed.

Sin pivoted slowly toward Patience, steeling himself against the hurt he'd surely see written across her face.

"And to think I have been dwelling on your

financial troubles for days." Her chin lifted a notch. "I was searching for any way to help you and your family. I even pondered the notion of our marriage. My dowry would more than repair your estate coffers, but a liar?" She shook her head back and forth, her eyes never leaving his. "I could never promise my hand, my heart, my future to a man who can so easily deceive a lady."

He'd been overwhelmed with thoughts of home and his people, while she'd been considering giving up everything she knew for a man who was deceiving her.

"I had no intention of—"

"Save your falsehoods for another, *Sin*." She hissed his name as if it were the foulest curse word she knew. "You would be wise to have your wounds cleansed and wrapped to prevent infection."

He was going to say he had no intention of asking her to make such a sacrifice—for him or his family— but she spun away from him before he could beg her to listen. They could not part in such a manner.

As she stalked across the warehouse toward the door, Sin followed, determined to catch her before she left. He had to explain, let her know he'd also searched for a way to keep his promise to her, but he hadn't come up with any solutions.

"Patience?"

Patience halted, causing Sin to nearly collide with her.

"What are you doing here?"

Sin had been so focused on Patience's retreating back that he hadn't seen the man stepping in their path until they were forced to stop or step around him.

"I asked what you are doing in Seven Dials." The Earl of Desmond appeared furious enough to spit fire. "Donaldson said you'd departed with Merit and Valor. Where are those scoundrels?"

"Father—I—well," Patience stammered. "What are *you* doing here?"

"Not that it is any of your concern, but I noted a wager at White's. The Earl of St. Seville to fight Parsons, and I thought to arrive early and talk some sense into the man," he said, his narrowed stare meeting Sin's where he stood behind Patience. "I arrived too late. But I will have your answer, young lady."

Patience's shoulders collapsed a bit, and she lowered her chin in shame.

"I have been attending Southlund's House…training the earl," she confessed.

Sin felt the weight of her secret even as her father's face clouded with confusion.

"You are here to *support* St. Seville?" Desmond's stare widened in shock, just as Sin's would have two days prior if anyone had told him Lady Patience Lane would not only stand in his corner but also teach him Ivory Bess's famed maneuvers. "After all these years of sending me to unsavory areas all across London to distribute your pamphlets. After all the friends I've lost because of my stance on pugilism. It has all been a fool's errand?"

Suddenly, it was only Desmond, Patience, and him in the warehouse as everything and everyone around them faded.

Patience's dedication and passion wasn't a fool's errand…had never been such.

The earl must know that.

"It is my fault, my lord," Sin offered. "It was I who persuaded Pat—Lady Patience—to instruct me. She did not want to. I am responsible for bringing her to Seven Dials."

Lady Patience's downcast expression at her father's fury made it necessary for Sin to speak what he did. Would Patience know his intent was never to lie to her but instead to protect her from the hard decision he'd made?

His words fell on deaf ears. Desmond never once

took his stare from Patience, not even to acknowledge or reprimand Sin for daring to bring Patience to the West End.

"We can speak about it on the way home." Desmond gestured for Patience to proceed him from the building. "St. Seville, you would be wise not to set foot in Southlund's House again. You are not welcome at Marsh Manor either." The earl glanced from Patience and past Sin. "Good day, Coventry. Holstrom."

Patience swept past Sin and turned back to where her father waited.

Could it be that she deliberated if she wanted to accompany her father home?

He saw the question in her clouded eyes, more blue than gray in that instant.

Sin would never ask her to choose between him and her family. There would only ever be one choice for her. It was the same for him. They would always choose their family.

When he'd lied to Patience, it had been because of his responsibility to his family and the future of his estate.

He wanted to tell her it was all right, that she owed him nothing. There shouldn't be any confliction when it came to deciding between Sin and her father. There was no decision to be made. Her allegiance belonged to Desmond.

But Patience didn't glance back again, only strode past her father and out the door into the brisk, cold night.

It shouldn't matter, but her departure wounded him far more than any thrown fist could. It wasn't something that caused him injury that would heal with time. When Patience left, she took a piece of him with her.

What remained was far more painful than the bruises to his chest and face and the cuts on his knuckles.

Something no amount of time or distance could heal.

It would remain open, broken without chance of repair.

Perhaps it was for the best. His injuries from pugilism would heal, but to take from Patience the life she deserved was something Sin could never do.

A hand clapped Sin's back, sending a sharp burst of pain down into his legs and up his neck.

"Well, St. Seville," Holstrom said, standing at his side. "You cannot say I did not caution you against entangling yourself with Desmond and his sharp-tongued shrew of a daughter."

Sin turned swiftly, his clenched fist slamming into Holstrom's nose, sending fresh blood cascading down the lord's chin and onto his pristine, white linen shirt and neckcloth.

"Never—I mean never—shall Lady Patience's name or any reference to her or her family cross your lips again. Let that be my words of caution to you, Holstrom."

Holstrom held his nose, blood oozing through his fingers and he stared at Sin with rounded, shocked eyes as the color drained from his face.

Before his temper flared any hotter and his fury took the small amount of control Sin still held, he elbowed past Holstrom, making certain his fists remained by this sides as he moved toward the Earl of Coventry, who stood several feet away.

"St. Seville?" Coventry asked, his brow raised in question, and a smirk curving the corners of his mouth upward.

"Can I trouble you for the use of your carriage?" Sin rumbled.

He didn't wait for an answer but stepped around the earl toward the back door of the warehouse. It was best if Sin didn't encounter anyone else who might disparage Lady Patience or her family—for the slim strand of control he held would surely snap.

Although that breakage was nothing compared to his heart.

CHAPTER 16

PATIENCE LEAPT FROM the carriage and raced into the house the moment the driver opened the door. The front of their townhouse was alight and waiting for Patience and her father to return. The cold night air bit into her cheeks, sending a shiver down her spine. Her refusal to speak to or even look at her father for the endless ride home was childish and would only serve to delay the inevitable coming argument.

But there was no other way for Patience to hide the agony and embarrassment she felt at Sin's deception. Her father would see through the anger she was using as a front to mask the turmoil within her.

Sin had lied to her, unequivocally and without remorse.

And Patience had taken him at his word. Never before had she believed any man, besides her father, when they told her something of such consequence. Even Merit and Valor were not above her questioning their every action and word—and the object of her scorn if they were proven dubious in any way.

But the Earl of St. Seville—no, *Sin*—had broken through her resolve, causing her to lower her guard.

Drop the wall she'd constructed after her mother's death when society had spurned her due to her strongly held convictions.

Patience kept her head lowered as she hurried through the foyer and past the main stairs. She would be easily found if she went directly to her room, and she'd run the risk of catching her maid turning down her bed for the night.

She'd misguidedly believed Sin had listened to her…and heard every word. More than that, she'd fooled herself into thinking that he *cared* for her.

Foolish.

Childish.

Gullible, silly girl.

Were those the many things Sin and his cohorts—Coventry and Holstrom—jested about after she left? Perhaps they'd adjourned to their gentlemen's club and were even now spreading news of the hilarity of her actions. All of London would know she wasn't only a champion for a cause that no one believed in, but also that she had been foolish enough to think herself falling in love with a man who was doing nothing but lie to her. They'd spent days together at Southlund's training. She'd risked her father's disappointment at discovering her activities, and all because she thought something—she wasn't certain what to call it, friendship, more than friendship?—had developed between them. She'd spoken of her mother and the despair surrounding her passing.

Had Sin gone so far as to create a ruse in an attempt to fool Patience into training him in the art of pugilism?

If so, she was more simpleminded than even she'd thought.

And now her father knew of her failings.

She regretted abandoning her work to abolish pugilism far more now knowing her father's disappointment in her.

Voices echoed behind her, but she kept moving, her feet tangling in the hem of her skirt for a brief moment. She'd thought the air outside abrasive, and the stale air of the carriage stifling; however, the walls of her home were not the sanctuary she'd expected. Her lungs contracted and expanded in time with her pulsing heart.

Her breaths fled her on ragged gasps.

She knew what was coming, and she'd be damned if her father or her maid would witness it.

Patience was about to cry…over a man she barely knew.

Blessedly, she reached the library and cast herself out the veranda door, stepping onto the terrace. However, she didn't stop there, she continued on into the garden. The area her mother had cherished, especially after the countess had promised her husband she'd no longer enter the ring. Patience had watched her mother toil away in the roses for hours. She'd been meticulous when inspecting each bud, selecting the perfect blossoms to be snipped and collected for display in the house. Before the previous day at Southlund's House, it was the gardens Patience sought out whenever she longed to feel closer to her mother.

At the moment, Patience wasn't fleeing to the garden to be close to her mother, to feel her presence. The last thing she wanted was to be reminded of the sport that had taken her mother and led Sin to deceive her.

No, she needed to be alone. In the gardens, no one disturbed Patience, just as they'd allowed the countess her solitude when she worked among her roses.

The late hour had brought dew that clung to the grass, and it dampened her skirt as she slowed to a walk, turning her face to the cloud-covered night sky. The breeze held the familiar scent of rain, necessary to wash away the soot and smog that clung to most of London.

The clouds slinking across the inky sky made the moon and stars invisible. Patience embraced the chill, allowing it to wash over her as the tears came, slowly sliding down her cheeks. She allowed the wind and her tears to wipe away the muddled mess she'd created of her life.

Patience turned slowly in a circle until she faced away from her house and any unwitting observers within.

In recent years, she'd turned into a woman she didn't recognize, crusading for a cause that she wasn't certain anyone but she and her father understood. She'd cast every person in her life—and those she met—into places of insignificance and ultimately forgotten about them, knowing she would, at some point, leave them behind in pursuit of her primary goal.

When had that happened?

But the Earl of St. Seville had broken through her guard that night at Lord Holstrom's soirée. Or had it happened before that when Patience had happened upon him, stripped to the waist in Merit's private chamber?

They'd both been vulnerable in that moment. She gowned in nothing but her white shift, and Sin bloodied without his shirt and jacket.

She'd hidden her vulnerabilities by cowering behind her convictions and her *work*.

The foolish, bloody pamphlets.

Her fists clenched at her sides until her nails cut through her gloves and into the palms of her hands.

It had taken only the sight of Sin—and his kind words in Holstrom's hall—and Patience had all but forgotten the one passion she'd clung to since her mother's death. She'd gone so far as to reenter Southlund's House.

She'd lied to her father.

Perhaps she'd lied to herself, as well.

A frigid droplet of rain landed on her upturned

face, mingling with her warm tears.

Her years of caution in regards to pugilism, the hours spent speaking with fighters, profiteers, and the printing of her pamphlets had made no difference, except to make her an outcast among those who should see her as their equal…a peer.

She'd toted her self-righteous message to all and sundry.

And then had quickly forgotten it all when she saw Sin's need.

In the last five years, Patience had made certain that not a single member of society got to know her. She'd hidden behind her *work*. But why?

If Sin had taught her anything, it was that she'd been right to hide, both herself and her heart. The hurt at discovering Sin's lies wounded her as deeply as her mother's passing had.

It was a betrayal to her mother and her memory to even think this way. Comparing the death of her most loved and cherished relative to the lies of a man she'd met only a week prior? She wasn't only an insufferable person, she was also an ungrateful daughter. In her selfish need to champion her mother's death, Patience had knowingly sent her father into harm's way, night after night, distributing her pamphlets. Worse yet, his reclusive nature had been Patience's doing, as well. Each time he went out on her fool's errands, he relived the loss of his countess.

It was his undoing.

Patience finally allowed the sobs to leave her, breaking the silence of the night…and doing nothing to alleviate her pain.

An agony she had no right to feel.

Her father was worthy of his continued sorrow. Sin was deserving of his all-consuming need to save his family and his people. Even the men and women who chose prizefighting as their means of crawling out of the deplorable circumstances of their birth had the right to seek a better future.

Damnation, if a person enjoyed the sport, who was Patience to fight, kick, and scream at them to change their interests?

Her mother had never given up on pugilism, even after she retired from fighting. She taught at Southlund's and passed her passion for the sport on to another generation of pugilists. Including Patience. There had been a time when Patience knew no greater joy than seeing the smile on her mother's face when she executed an advanced move in the ring or when she bested her sparring partner.

She'd taken something that had been a source of pride for her family and turned it into something so vile she felt compelled to shout her warnings from the rooftops.

In her single-minded pursuit, she'd even pushed her siblings away.

Her sisters, Temperance and Verity, scrambled to wed and be away from Marsh Manor, and Merit and Valor spent increasingly large spans of time away from their townhouse. And her father remained in his study when he wasn't at his club.

Patience had done this to her family.

She'd thought she was helping others, stopping them from suffering what her family had, but instead, she was making it impossible for her family to exist in one home.

Could it be that she'd been utterly wrong? Maybe not in her belief that brawling was a danger but that life itself could ever be completely safe.

Tonight, she'd pushed Sin away, likely forever, and all because she didn't see that his reasons were as important or worthy as her own.

"What have I done?" she demanded of the sky above.

In response, the clouds overhead parted and the midnight moon shone brightly.

CHAPTER 17

IN THE AFTERMATH of his confrontation with Holstrom—and in his hurry to depart Seven Dials—Sin had paid no heed to the two men who followed him from the warehouse to Coventry's waiting carriage in the alley. Due to his rage over the circumstances, Sin didn't bother glancing about when he paused to put on his shirt, followed by his jacket. He was prepared for any confrontation to come. In his need to see Lady Patience, and in his anger at himself for hurting her, Sin hadn't noticed the two men climbing into the carriage after him. And as the pain from his injuries began to draw at the edges of his mind, and the exhilaration of the fight subsided, Sin finally glanced up from his place in the carriage to see the two dark-haired men sitting across from him.

Their mirrored glowers and crossed arms did nothing to clear Sin's fogging mind, even as his thoughts swirled around, demanding the driver to deliver him to the Earl of Desmond's townhouse with the haste of a thousand wild horses.

Certainly, most men would be concerned when faced by two adversaries whose menacing glares in no way promised friendship. However, not even both men combined could equal Sin's weight, and even with his injuries from the prizefight, he was certain the two men would not prove a threat to him. If they thought to attack him and take his prize purse, they would have done it before entering the carriage.

The minutes had ticked by as their hostile, almost ferocious, stares hadn't diminished in the least.

However, the pain of his injuries—had he broken his hand or suffered bruising to his back?—had cleared his mind and brought an acute awareness to his surroundings—and his need to quicken his journey across London.

Each time Sin called to the driver to make haste, one or both of the men shouted for the driver to remain halted. The bolder of the two kept his hand on the carriage door latch, daring Sin to make a move to exit.

Sin chuckled. If the men wanted a fight, Sin had enough pent-up aggressive growing inside him to take on the men without a second thought. If they were here to pinch his winnings and make off into the night, then he wished they'd get on with their business and leave him to his next task.

"May I help you, gentlemen?" he asked, his voice level and even, his gaze moving from one man to the other. They appeared vaguely familiar, and Sin wondered if they'd passed in the halls of the Albany or perhaps they were members of Coventry's exclusive club. Their lapels were devoid of a golden *W*, which dispelled the notion that they were aligned with the Wicked Earls' Club. "Are you here for something, or are you simply in need of transport back to London proper?"

"What is your business with Lady Patience Lane?" It was the man holding the door closed, preventing Sin from departing, who spoke. In proper lighting, the pair would be hard to tell apart, and without a proper introduction, Sin could only note the lines on the man's face to indicate that he was the elder of the two men.

"That is none of your concern," Sin retorted. If they were simply more men thinking to warn him away from Patience, they'd picked the wrong day to issue their cautionary stories. And if either thought to disparage the woman's name, they would see the same fate as Holstrom had. "If you will excuse me—"

"I would have to say it is exactly our concern, my lord." This came from the younger man. Sin quickly realized why the men appeared familiar, though he was confident that they'd never met. "You will answer my brother's question. Now."

Knowing the men were not present to cause him serious harm should have eased Sin, but it only served to fill him with guilt over what Patience was suffering through. These men were her family—her brothers, if Sin weren't mistaken. If anyone deserved to know Sin's intentions with Lady Patience, it was the gentlemen sitting across from him.

"My business with Lady Patience isn't about *business* at all." It was the truth. Never had Sin thought of Patience in a business sense. He hadn't met her with any nefarious notions in mind; in fact, he'd wondered at her intentions when she stumbled upon him that night in her home. "We met not long ago, and it doesn't pain me to admit…I care for her greatly."

"And yet you do the one thing that will crush her feelings?" the younger man scoffed.

However, the tension drained from the man next to him. "I am Valor, and this is Merit."

"Patience's brothers," Sin continued for them.

Merit, the young brother, asked, "Is it so obvious?"

"Dark complexion, dark hair, and eyes that change from blue to grey with your mood and the lighting—no, the resemblance isn't obvious at all."

"You left the fight in a bit of a rush," Valor

continued, re-crossing his arms as if remembering why he'd waylaid Sin's coach. "Where are you headed?"

"Most likely the same place you are," Sin offered, crossing his own arms and pegging the men with his coolest stare.

"Do not think to know where we are headed, my lord," Merit threw back. Of the pair, Sin thought Patience was much like this young man: fiery and passionate with a healthy dose of indignation.

"I planned to go to your townhouse and beg Patience to see me."

"Did you not hear our father?" Valor retorted. "You have been banned from both Southlund's House and Marsh Manor."

"And if I do not heed Desmond's words?" Sin asked, lifting his chin to stare down at the men. "Will the pair of you attempt to stop me?"

"Depends," Merit offered, but he'd relaxed ever so slightly since he entered the coach and sat across from Sin.

"On…?"

"Whether you mean to cause Patience more hurt," Valor said. "We do not take kindly to anyone harming our sister, as I'm sure you can understand."

"I do," Sin agreed. "However, I can assure you, I never meant to hurt Patience in the first place."

"Be that as it may,"—Merit pushed up straight in his seat—"you did cause her grief. So acutely she made a spectacle of herself before half of London. What about her reputation? Do you think she will ever find a suitable man to wed now?"

It was Sin's turn to scoff at the question. "Patience doesn't care what society thinks of her, and marriage is not high on her list of priorities." When both men returned to their menacing stares, Sin continued, "Is it possible I know your sister and her wishes better than the pair of you?"

He glanced between the brothers, a measure of satisfaction settling over him. Let them speak against his words, all three of them knew Sin was correct.

"Marsh Manor," Valor shouted, thumping his fist on the side of the carriage. Without delay, the driver called to the horses, and they were off. "We are well aware Patience has little respect for society and what they deem proper; however, she does respect you, St. Seville—or do you prefer Sin?"

"St. Seville suits adequately," he grunted and waited for Valor to continue.

"In all the years since our mother's passing, Patience has never entered Southlund's House. Yet, you, St. Seville, convinced her to go to a place she swore never to so much as set eyes on again. If that is not respect, I do not know what is."

"It is apparent that our sister cares for you, as well," Merit admitted grudgingly. "Now *we* must decide what to do about that."

We? Did they think to stop him from seeing Patience?

The men would have a hell of a time following through with that plan. Or perhaps they meant to forbid Patience from having anything to do with Sin.

The carriage hit a bump in the street, sending the brothers colliding into one another. Sin, however, had been prepared for the rough travel and he kept his seat. Streetlamps shone through the glass of the windows, signaling that they'd traveled far enough from Seven Dials to slow their speed.

"Tell me, St. Seville, how did you convince Patience to return to Southlund's?"

"It was she who offered to train me after seeing how deplorably I lost my first prizefight."

Valor drew back. "You expect us to believe that?"

"She was helping me," Sin confessed, turning his palms up. He had nothing to hide. Valor and Merit would hear it all eventually. "I am in London to save my family from ruin. Our coffers are empty, and my estate and people are suffering. If I do not win, I will have nothing to return home with. My land will lay fallow, and my people will starve. That is the reason Patience offered to help me."

The men looked at one another, some silent communication passing between them before they turned back to Sin with matching grins.

"You care for Patience?" Valor demanded. "More than using her to win enough funds to run off back to your estate?"

Sin nodded. "Without a doubt."

"And what do you plan to say to our sister if you are allowed to see her again?" Merit continued.

Sin hadn't thought through what he was going to say. He'd foolishly believed that if Patience agreed to see him—and Desmond allowed him into their home—the words would come.

His shoulders sagged. "I will tell her exactly how I feel about her…everything, including my plans to remain in London as long as possible to be near her. It is where she belongs, among those who know and love her." If their time at Southlund's House had taught Sin anything, it was that leaving London—and Patience behind—would rip his heart wide open.

"We can get you into the house," Merit said

"After that, it is up to you," Valor finished.

IF PATIENCE'S BROTHERS had warned Sin that their grand plan included sneaking him in through the back gardens and instructing him to scale the townhouse wall to the window Merit would prop open for him to enter, he would have told them to save their breaths. Instead, Sin listened intently as Coventry's carriage stopped in the mews behind Marsh Manor.

Sin glanced at the window, pleased to see that the light drizzle that had started earlier had stopped. He would not have to face the harrowing rose bushes with their pointed thorns and the slick siding of the house as he climbed—and fear losing his grip and falling into the waiting bushes.

Merit pointed up at the house, candles lighting several windows on both the main level and the second story. "My window is that one—"

"I know which is yours," Sin said, cutting off the man before realizing his folly.

"How, exactly, do you know which one is my room?" Merit asked, as serious as an inquisitor as he turned to face Sin.

Sin debated how much to share, but decided it could only serve to strengthen this support if they heard the truth of his first meeting with Patience. "During my first fortnight in London, your father happened upon me in an alley where I'd been set upon by a thief." There was little reason to share that Coventry had arranged the entire episode, for it would only lead to questions he didn't have time to answer. "He rescued me and brought me here to be seen to by your family physician."

"You did not answer my question…"

Sin had to admire the man's perceptiveness. "Desmond had me wait in your room. I had no intention of allowing the good doctor to examine me and so, after being caught by Patience, I escaped out your window and down into the gardens…narrowly missing those wild rose bushes."

"She caught you how—"

"You did what—"

Both Merit and Valor spoke at the same time, and Sin chuckled at their comical expressions. Valor, ever the eldest, was affronted, while Merit's eyes widened with utter shock.

"How is this the first time we are hearing of this?" Valor demanded.

"It is not a situation that needs to be discussed for fear of being overheard." Merit shoved at his brother and gestured at the window and Coventry's driver above. "We can discuss this later, perhaps in private. Mayhap you can invite us to your club, St. Seville."

"My club?" Whatever did the men speak of? Sin no more had a *club* than he did coins to plant crops on Brownsea.

"You know…" Merit nodded at Sin's jacket. "The Wicked Earls' Club."

"I cannot—"

"Come now, my lord," Valor prodded. "As soon as I inherit the Desmond earldom, I will petition Coventry for membership. But until then…"

"I meant I am not part of Coventry's group," Sin sighed. "The earl is a friend, *was* a friend of my father's. He is helping me while I'm in London."

Valor rolled his eyes, and Merit stared expectantly.

"I am sorry I cannot be of help." Sin turned to glance out the window as one of the lights on the second floor extinguished. "I think it is best we hurry before Lady Patience retires to her bed."

"Of course." Valor pulled the latch, and the door opened. "We will drive round to the front and hurry up to Merit's chambers to open the window for you."

Sin nodded and stepped out of the carriage, his boots landing in a puddle of mud from the recent rain. Glancing up, he saw that the clouds were pulling away, and the moon shone through, lighting the path in front of him. The last time he'd been in the Desmond gardens, the night had been pitch black.

"Good luck, St. Seville," Valor called as the carriage started down the alleyway and out of sight.

Sin would need more than mere luck to convince

Patience to hear what he had to say. She was justified in despising him. He'd deceived her and had prayed his lies would remain hidden until he fled London…like a coward.

Pulling the collar on his coat up to block the breeze from touching his exposed neck, Sin ducked his head and started for Lady Patience's townhouse and the climb that would either see him injured in the rose bushes or standing before a woman he had no right to care about.

The climb down had been simple enough as he'd found foot and handholds readily enough, but going up, after his hours of fighting, seemed daunting and risky.

Lady Patience was worth the risk, though. If she forgave him, he would use the purse prize he'd won in Seven Dials to keep his people provided for until spring came and then he'd find another way—something besides pugilism—to bring his estate and people back from ruin.

The mud sloshed under his boots, and a single cloud drifted over the moon, momentarily darkening the garden before him.

The house wasn't far away, but it seemed, no matter how fast he walked, he'd never reach it—or Patience. Were she and Desmond still arguing? Was she preparing for bed? Had she already slipped beneath the covers, her eyes heavy with tears?

Sin exited the muddy path that wound through the garden's shrubbery to the expanse of lawn that separated him from the townhouse beyond.

His steps faltered when he caught sight of a lone figure in the middle of an open area.

A woman.

It was far too late for a servant to be about the gardens, and the temperatures were plummeting as morning approached.

His heart knew the woman before his mind did.

Her face was turned toward the night sky, and as the clouds moved, revealing the moon once more, the twinkling twilight rained down on her. Her dark brown hair, still tied back at the base of her neck, shimmered. Her lithe body shook, and Sin realized Patience was sobbing. Not loud, wailing bursts of anguish but soft gut-wrenching weeping.

And it was all because of him.

He drew closer but remained quiet. He was intruding on a private moment, something he wasn't supposed to witness. Yet Sin would rather cast himself from the rocky cliffs of Brownsea Island and into the roaring, twisting, churning ocean below than take his eyes off Patience.

There was a startling beauty there despite her anguish.

Not her pain, never that, but in the way the hurt seeped from her as she cried, almost as if it left her and escaped into the night. He wanted to ask her the secret to letting it all go, to accepting the things you had no power over and moving forward.

He had no doubt that that was exactly what she was doing out in the garden all alone.

She was letting go of the past—her past. Her mother's illness, her father's despair, and her own desperate need to right all of society's wrongs.

Patience had needed this solitary moment, while Sin had misguidedly thought to right all his family's trouble alone—yet, he'd needed help. *Her* help.

Slowly, her shoulders straightened, and her chin lowered, and her tear-streaked face came into view. Her eyes were squeezed tight. To keep out the few wayward raindrops or to hold tight to whatever her mind's eye saw behind her lids, Sin didn't know.

He *did* know that he wanted to be there with her…to help her as she'd done for him.

To make right his part of the pain he'd caused.

She sighed—long and deep—and Sin's heart fractured into a thousand pieces.

How had he ever thought he could survive without her, leave her and London behind...that ever a day existed he could forget a woman such as Lady Patience Lane?

CHAPTER 18

PATIENCE BREATHED IN deeply and exhaled slowly, begging the ache in her chest to subside; however, it persisted. Would likely stay for some time, much like those endless months following her mother's passing. Perhaps the ache would never fully disappear, and the piece of her heart that hadn't left this life with her mother would remain with Sin wherever he journeyed.

The tragic part was that he'd never even know what he'd taken from her.

No, not taken.

She had freely given a portion of herself to him, foolishly thinking he'd nurture and cherish it. She'd outgrown the notion everyone wanted to—or could—be saved, despite her best intentions. If anything, her time in society had taught her that. But she'd allowed her guard to fall.

And this was her punishment.

How could she truly believe she'd given him a portion of herself and yet, never had their lips touched? And now their time together had ended without so much as even a chaste kiss.

It was time she faced it head-on, dealt with her father's disappointment, made amends with her siblings and decided what direction her life would take in the coming years. Would she move to her family's country estate and withdraw from society altogether? Could she live a content life without having a cause to champion? Maybe it was long past time she learned.

Patience would not miss London, certainly not; however, she would mourn the distance between herself and her family. Would they visit during the holidays or invite her to return to town to spend the Christmastide celebration with them?

What was the deep of winter like on the island of Brownsea? Did the tides rise? Was the land shrouded by the same gray darkness as London? Did they dine on fish instead of duck and pheasant? Were their soups heavy with crustaceans and fresh vegetables?

Was the crisp breeze from the sea preferable to the coal-tainted air in town?

All things Patience would never know and would be best to keep from dwelling on.

Once she opened her eyes and returned to the house, her moment of mourning would be at an end. Dwelling on something one could not change was a waste of time, though it had taken Patience five long years to realize that fact.

The cold breeze licked at her cheeks, and her nose tingled.

The night grew late, and Patience needed to return inside before the chill settled in her. With any luck, her father would have retired to his private chambers or locked himself away in his study, and she could slip through the house unnoticed. In the morning, she would throw herself at his mercy. No matter what it took, Patience would make things right with her father…she would make it right for everyone. Perhaps she owed Lord Holstrom and his wife an apology, as well as the other gentlemen of the *ton* she'd harassed over the years.

But not tonight—now, she would retire, though sleep would certainly not drag her down into its inky depths and banish her misdeeds.

Patience hesitantly opened her eyes, the dim night almost too bright after the darkness behind her lids. The sting was a welcome distraction from the emptiness that echoed inside her.

Too quickly, the pain subsided, and her vision focused.

She wasn't alone in the garden.

"Sin?" Her hushed tone barely traveled farther than her parted lips. "What are you doing here?"

The sight of him, still raw and ravaged from his fight, burned into her memory. She'd never thought to see him again, had never dreamed he'd come to her. Or that her heart would soar at the sight of him, even in his ragged condition.

He was before her in the blink of an eye, and he swept her into his arms—his powerful, comforting embrace—pulling her body against his. Every muscle in his chest and abdomen pressed solidly against her softer flesh as if no barrier lay between them.

Caution prickled within her. "You are injured, Sin. Did the physician examine your hands before you left Seven Dials? I can summon Dr.—"

"Shhhh." His breath fogged between them. "Do not worry about me. It is you who is hurt, and I am the cause."

Her stomach fluttered at his words, the emptiness within her suddenly filling as if it had never been as his lips stopped a hairsbreadth from hers. Only a mere tilt of her head and their mouths would meet. Desire pooled at her core, urging her to move and bring them together, but she hesitated when he spoke once more.

"I never meant to cause you pain, Patience," he

confessed, his brown eyes locking on hers in the night. "However, I allowed my own needs to preclude everything else." He shook his head, their bodies breaking apart. "No, I will not make excuses for my deplorable behavior and cowardly actions."

Cowardly? Sin was the furthest thing from that.

"Do not say such things," Patience said, her hand finding his and squeezing it gently. His knuckles likely ached. "You are devoted to saving your family, that is a far more worthy cause than my irrational belief that I could end a sport my mother loved. I was trying to change my past, which makes no sense, while you…you were attempting to make a better future for yourself and so many others."

"You cannot say that all you do is for the past," he countered.

"Yes, I can, and no matter what I do, I cannot bring her back. I am only pushing those who love me away." She shook her head, remembering the look of utter disbelief and injury on her father's face. "I was—am—selfish."

Her voice trembled, and Patience hated herself for it.

She was the coward. She was the one who couldn't accept her past and move on.

"I gave you no option but to lie," she sighed, focusing her stare on the ground between them. "I foolishly believed that my need to educate fighters about pugilism was a worthier pursuit than your mission to save your family and estate. You must think me a silly half-wit."

"No." He pulled his hand free from hers, and Patience wilted. "I think you are brave and overcome with compassion. Not many women would face the wrath and scorn of society for any cause, let alone for a sport so vastly popular."

"But I persuaded you to agree to my terms."

"I willingly agreed to your terms merely to keep seeing you," Sin confessed. "Do not think you put me at a disadvantage. Besides, I broke at least two of them, and you have not collected on the third."

Patience's brow furrowed as she thought back to her demands. The first was that he would listen and heed her advice. Sin had certainly broken that rule. He would win his freedom from Holstrom, and they would work together to find a solution that did not end with Sin suffering head injuries. While he'd voiced his agreement for future matches, Sin hadn't fought any yet. But it would be selfish of her, once again, to beg him to abstain from prizefighting.

The third...the meaning behind his name.

"Sin," he said, as if reading her thoughts. "My younger sister, Juliette, could not say Sinclair as a babe. Sinbar...Sintar...Sincar. After months of corrections, she settled on Sin."

"It was not because of your devilishly handsome good looks?" Patience teased.

"You think I am handsome?" he retorted, his eye widening in mock surprise.

She ignored his question but couldn't hold back her smile. "I am pleased to know it was not given due to an adverse demeanor."

"A handsome devil with a tendency for wicked behavior." He rubbed his stubbly chin as a wayward lock of hair hung over one eye.

"I think you would be best described as a seafaring pirate with a delightful demeanor."

How had he banished her dour mood so readily?

For a brief few minutes, Patience was able to forget about the dire situation awaiting her in the house. Her heart didn't ache as it had when the rain had pelted her upturned face. She wasn't dwelling on the thought of never seeing Sin again.

He stood before her, towered over her. And she

was content to realize that his presence made her feel safe and cared for. Not overpowered and ignored.

She'd thought Sin had once and for all crushed her hopes for the future and would depart London with a piece of her heart hidden on his person.

Could it be that did not have to be her fate?

"When I told you I pondered offering myself to you in marriage—along with my sizeable dowry—I was gravely serious." She'd dispelled the light, jesting air that had settled around them; however, Patience could not allow Sin to depart without knowing what her heart held, even if his feelings did not mirror her own.

"You would do that to keep me from fighting?" he asked.

"Partly." Nothing in her years of getting in the fighting ring or going after the wealthiest, titled men of the peerage to plead her case had prepared her for this moment. She sensed his next question before he spoke the words—and she knew he deserved the truth.

He drew closer to her, his warmth a welcome reprieve from the night. "And the other part?"

"Because I cannot imagine a future without you," she murmured, embarrassment staining her cheeks. "I know you likely think that just another naïve notion. We have known one another for such a short time, however—"

"I have never thought any such thing." His hand cupped her cheek, turning her eyes to his, and she swam in their warmth, nestled against the heat of his palm. Unease and anticipation burrowed within her when she saw her own desire and longing reflected in his eyes. "I could not accept your offer, no matter how much I longed to. London is where you belong, while I belong on Brownsea Island, close to my people and the ocean. I cannot ask you to leave your home, just as I know you would never ask me to remain in town."

"And if I told you there is nothing left for me

here?" she challenged.

"I would disagree, vehemently." His fingers caressed her cheek. "What of your family?"

Patience scoffed. "I love my family, but I have hurt them all with my crusade. My father has lost friends. My siblings…I can only image what my actions have done to them."

"They love you."

"As I love them, but even before you arrived, I had set my course on leaving London," she said. "Perhaps retiring to my father's country estate."

"What in heavens would you do there?"

It was the same thing Patience had pondered. "Teach in the village schoolhouse. Mayhap take up tending the garden—my mother loved it so. Or I could learn a new sport. Archery is acceptable for women."

"And what of marriage?" His eyes narrowed. "And love?"

Patience chuckled. "You know I am not particularly fond of any man who's made my acquaintance. And love?" Her chest seized. "I shall come to love the country, the villagers, and perhaps a quiet existence. I will take up reading or science."

"You could do those things anywhere," Sin mused.

"I suppose I could." Was he agreeing to her idea of moving to the country, or was he saying she should remain in town? "However, I do know London is not the place I wish to live."

"Brownsea has gardens and a wonderful village brimming with kind people."

"Brownsea?" Patience's heart stopped before stuttering several times. "You cannot mean…"

The words died on her lips. If she said the wrong thing, what would Sin think? However, remaining silent didn't seem right either.

"Lady Patience Lane." He paused, clearing his throat, and Patience's entire body tensed. He hadn't been about to say what she longed to hear.

A sob threatened to betray her disappointment. Could she survive another parting like the one in Seven Dials? At least she'd been the one to walk away then, and Sin had been made to watch her retreating back. This time, it would be Patience frozen to her spot as Sin walked away and out of her life.

In that moment, Patience understood the pain her father had faced when her mother's illness had progressed, and she passed away. She wanted to wrap her arms around Sin and hold him so tightly that he would be unable to leave. She would tell him anything, live her life doing his bidding if only he would promise never to leave her. Never to condemn her to a fate similar to her father's.

An empty shell.

Without thought, Patience grabbed Sin's shoulders and pulled him toward her at the same time she stood on her tiptoes.

"Sin." She closed her eyes and pressed her lips to his, silently begging him not to pull away. It was a sensation of new beginnings, of longings always denied. His mouth was tender against hers as the draw to be closer to him, to wrap herself in his warmth, became inescapable. There was no room for doubt or uncertainty.

Her heart soared ever higher when Sin wrapped his arms around her, pulling her so close to his body that her bosom pressed against his chest. The hammering of her heart kept pace with his as their lips melded.

Suddenly, her heart stopped, and her breath hitched. Sin, with her in this moment, was the only thing that mattered to Patience. Not her father, not her past, not the many questions that would follow this moment. None of it held any significance if Sin was not with her.

Patience's fingers grasped his coat, refusing to

allow him to move away.

The feeling inside her…the urgent desire to be close to Sin, would not be fleeting nor diminish with time. Even distance would not lessen her longings.

This was where Patience was meant to be, and it had nothing to do with London or the country or Brownsea.

It wasn't about a place but a person.

Her mother, Ivory Bess, had been her father's home…and Sin was hers.

Wherever he was, so would be her heart.

Too soon, Sin pulled back, cupping her face and bringing it close to his as Patience quivered, her legs straining from being on her tiptoes.

"Lady Patience Lane." This time, he didn't pause, nor did he look the least bit hesitant. "If the offer stands, I would be honored to take you away from London to Brownsea Island—as my wife and countess."

"But, I thought"—She sucked in a deep breath—"I thought you said…"

"I said I would never allow you to sacrifice your future to save my estate," he finished for her. "However, if you shall have me, I have no intention of wedding you for your dowry."

"It is all I can bring to the union."

"You could not be more wrong," he whispered, placing a gentle kiss on her lips. "You will bring hope to Brownsea. You will bring your passion for helping others. And you will bring love."

Patience's heart swelled at the mention of love. It was more than she'd ever dared to hope for.

"We shall return to my home and bring with us our love."

Patience reached forward with trembling fingers and brushed a lock of hair from his face, sweeping it behind his ear. "For your people?"

"Love for each other."

She'd known since the moment she agreed to return to Southlund's House—for him—that her heart was no longer her own. But daring to hope that he felt the same was something she hadn't allowed herself.

"Patience, I love you with a depth I never thought possible. A moment without you by my side would be an eternity of emptiness."

"I love you, too, Sinclair Chambers." She uttered his name for the first time, but it wasn't right. Even St. Seville didn't fit him properly. "Sin," she corrected.

Just as her father had fallen in love with a bonny lass from Seven Dials, so had Patience fallen in love with a Corinthian prizefighter. There was a certain poetic note to the entire situation. She was certain they would face their own trials and tribulations, but that was more preferable than a lifetime without Sin.

"St. Seville!" The sudden shout echoed across the garden, startling Patience from Sin's hold.

They both turned to see Valor leaning so far out Merit's window he was in jeopardy of falling into the overgrown rose thicket below.

"Whatever are you doing?" Patience shouted back. "Get back inside before you fall out."

"St. Seville. If you wed Patience, you will have no choice but to give Merit and I entrance to the Wicked Earls' Club. I will have it added to the betrothal agreement."

"What in heavens?" Patience turned her questioning stare to Sin.

He only shrugged, pressing his lips to her ear as he whispered, "They helped me back here, so I suppose I—*we*—owe them a small favor." He turned and smiled up at her brothers. "I will speak with Coventry and see what I can do."

"See that you do," Merit called over Valor's shoulder.

"I do not think it is a good idea at all, my lord,"

Patience mumbled for Sin's ears alone.

"I have no doubt it is a terrible idea; however, if it is in the betrothal agreement, I will agree to anything to have you."

"You have already proven that." Patience laughed, the sound echoing across the garden.

Above them, the window closed, and her brothers disappeared from view, leaving only Sin and Patience—and the growing desire that had blossomed the moment she spotted him bare-chested in her home.

Sin pulled her against him once more, and Patience didn't stop herself from throwing her arms around his neck.

She wanted this moment to last forever, this glimpse in time with the moon bright above and the air cold on her skin...with the promise of many more kisses to warm her.

CHAPTER 19

SIN GRINNED WIDELY as he read the betrothal contract on the table separating him from the Earl of Desmond—and flanked on both sides by Lady Patience's brothers, Merit and Valor. As promised, though most likely begrudgingly added by the earl, was a stipulation aimed at gaining some form of membership to the Wicked Earls' Club for Merit and Valor.

Some form of membership was a broad and vague term, and the Earl of Desmond had demanded, in a hushed whisper, that Sin only get his sons an invitation for a meal or two at the club and nothing more.

It was an easy enough promise to make—far simpler to keep than those he'd made to Lady Patience.

Sin glanced at the precisely written agreement one more time before dipping his quill into the ink pot at the right and signing his name.

Honestly, it didn't matter what he had to promise as long as Patience was to be his wife.

As if knowing he needed her close, Patience's light laughter sounded from across the room where she and her sisters were seated before the fire while the men handled important matters—or so the elder earl had stated. Sin, as well as Patience's entire family, was sheltered inside Marsh Manor as the rains from several days before turned into a torrential downpour that made travel outside the city impossible.

Sin glanced at Patience, not at all shocked to find her staring back at him.

Her dark locks hung in perfect curls down her back, the front pinned at her crown with a pearl hairpin. A rosy flush stained her cheeks, and Sin had the desperate urge to join her and her sisters to discover what they laughed about…and chuckle along with them.

Setting the quill aside, Sin pushed from his seat. "Will that be all, my lord?"

In only a fortnight, Sin had gone from having only himself to depend on to save his lands and his people, to realizing that not only would Patience be with him through the many hard years to come but also her family…who were soon to be part of his family, as well.

Desmond nodded. The exhaustion Sin had noted in the older man the night they met had seemingly disappeared. He even smiled before gesturing toward his three daughters, giving Sin permission to join them.

"Our work is done here, my boy," Desmond chuckled, collecting the paperwork.

Sin had thought it best for the Desmond solicitor to be present, but the earl, as well as Merit and Valor, hadn't thought it necessary. The betrothal agreement was standard, with no surprising terms besides that which dealt with the Wicked Earls' Club, and Patience's dowry was far more generous than Sin had expected. It was enough to see his estate returned to good standings with plenty left over for crops, repairs, and any needed equipment.

His refusal to accept such a large portion of the Desmond coffers went unheard, and the earl said he would find it difficult to bear living so far from his youngest child; however, knowing the St. Seville estate was in proper order would make, as he'd said, "an old man sleep well at night."

Turning toward the gathering of women, Sin came face-to-face with Patience as she strolled in his direction.

When had he realized that leaving her behind in London when he returned to Brownsea Island would never be an option for him? That night in his room at the Albany when she'd cleaned his wounds…their time at Southlund's House…when they'd journeyed to the Strand?

No, it was the moment she'd rushed to him in Bedford Square after Holstrom had turned his back on him and lifted him to his feet before helping him to her carriage.

Whatever had been lacking within him, the gaping hole he hadn't realized existed, had begun to fill in that moment.

Sin held out his arms, and Patience, without a second's hesitation, walked into them.

"Is it done?" she asked, setting her cheek against his chest. "Everything is signed?"

He nodded, placing a kiss to her forehead before tucking her head under his chin, no longer caring if the embrace was overly intimate. Everyone present wanted nothing but the best for Patience—and in quick order, she'd told her family exactly what would make her happy.

Sin, the Earl of St. Seville…and no one else.

It would be his life's mission to make certain he was worthy of both of her love and her sacrifices—each and every day.

"Are you certain this is what you desire?" he whispered. He knew he'd asked much of her: a life away from London and her family. "Brownsea is—"

"…where I will be happy. As long as you are there." She pulled back and gazed up at him. "I love you, Sin. I might've tried to fight it with everything I had, but my happiness, my heart, and my home are by your side."

Sin leaned down and placed his lips to hers, as if sealing her words and making his own promise in return. In that moment, it was only Patience who mattered. Her happiness and love guaranteed his future, and their future would be full of affection, adoration, and bliss.

EPILOGUE

SIN RECLINED ON the lawn bordering his family's home on Brownsea Island, Patience tucked by this side as they watched Juliette dance and sway on the sandy beach beyond. The temperature was overly warm for early summer, and he'd needed to reassure Patience that the weather would not always be so accommodating.

Theirs were not the only eyes watching Juliette frolic with abandon.

Desmond sat with Sin's mother on the terrace overlooking the lawns while the two caught up on all things society related. They'd been in Dorset, on the isle, for nearly a month, and still, the older pair never ran out of topics that interested them.

Perhaps it had been good for Desmond to make the journey with them.

Unfortunately, Valor and Merit were also in residence.

"Do stop that," Patience chided, slapping Sin's shoulder lightly.

"Stop what?" He glanced down, taking in her sun-kissed skin.

"You growled," she laughed.

"Well, I cannot say I relish the interest those two have taken in my dear sister," Sin retorted, watching as Valor danced beside Juliette, his knees rising high in a jig, all while Merit clapped along. "They pay her too much mind."

"Would you prefer they ignore her?" Patience questioned, pushing away from his chest to sit straight. She blocked the sun with her hand and watched the trio. "They do seem smitten, though, do they not?"

Sin would rather Patience's brothers kept their distance. "Juliette hasn't so much as had her debut Season yet."

"Which will change soon enough," Patience replied, leaning back into Sin and pressing her lips to his cheek.

"Not soon enough for me." Sin's uneasy chuckle was drowned out by the distant waves. "Tell me, my Countess of St. Seville, do you miss London?"

It was the main reason he'd thought they wouldn't suit: she'd been raised in town, and Sin much preferred the open expanse of life on Brownsea. Even after their nuptials a few weeks prior, Sin had held his breath in anticipation of her confession that island life was not to her liking, and that she found herself restless with nothing to occupy her time. Though she seemed happy enough.

He searched her face as she closed her eyes and tilted back her head once more, allowing the midday sun to caress her skin.

"I do not think it is possible to miss town when Brownsea is so beautiful, the people overly kind, and"— She tilted her face to his but didn't open her eyes, a smile playing on her lips—"leaving Brownsea would mean leaving my heart behind. Months ago, I was foolish enough to think that you held a piece of my heart, but now I've come to realize you hold all of it."

"So," he prodded, "you do not miss Marsh Manor,

society, and the endless entertainments?"

Her brow furrowed, and her eyes opened to meet his.

Why had he pressed the question?

"Everything I love—besides my sisters and their husbands—is here. Why would I miss London? Do we not have endless entertainments to keep us busy, my lord? The land is still in need of tilling and planting, the thatcher roofs in the village need mending, and it is my hope that a few of the children apply themselves to their studies with enough vigor to see them to University when the time comes."

Sin laughed as Patience gently squeezed his thigh. "You truly enjoy the day-to-day toils of life on Brownsea?"

"Of course. In fact, I think we could make better use of our time than watching my brothers attempt to woo your sister."

Leaping from the blanket, Sin started for the trio at the water's edge with Patience quickly by his side.

"Do stop, Sin," Patience called, taking hold of his arm. "My father, along with my brothers, will depart for London soon enough."

He allowed his beautiful wife to pull him back toward their blanket laid upon the green lawn. His mother and Desmond waved to them as they lowered themselves back to the soft earth, the scent of the ocean mingling with the fresh grass and the heat from the sun above. It reminded him of the night he'd promised himself to her, though it had been a full moon overhead. Their lips had met, and his arms had held her close as their bodies melted together as if they were made for one another.

"It was so very perfect," Patience cooed as if reading his mind.

"Yes, though we've shared many more moments since." But Sin knew that none could ever be so perfect

224 | *Christina McKnight*

as their first kiss. They'd had many chances before that night in her father's gardens, but it was as if destiny had kept them apart until the exact moment they both realized a future without the other would not be worth anything. "Like now"—Sin brought his face a mere inch from hers—"I could kiss you, for all to see, and—"

"You cannot kiss me here." Her breathless whisper told Sin it was exactly what she wanted him to do. "What will my father think? Or your sister?"

"That I am a man utterly in love with his wife," he said, placing a quick kiss on her pouting lips. "And that not only am I in love with her, but I will actively love her for all my days."

Laughter floated from the terrace, and a squeal of delight echoed from the water's edge, but Sin paid no mind to any of it.

His wife, her dark mane falling over her shoulder and cascading across his chest, was the object of his attention. Her grey-blue eyes sparkled with love and laughter, something that had been missing when they first met. Sin would do everything in his power to make certain the look shone brightly for the rest of their days.

WICKED EARLS' CLUB

Thank you for reading *Earl of St. Seville!*

If you enjoyed *Earl of St. Seville* be sure to write a brief review at any retailer.

Check out the other books in the Wicked Earls' Club

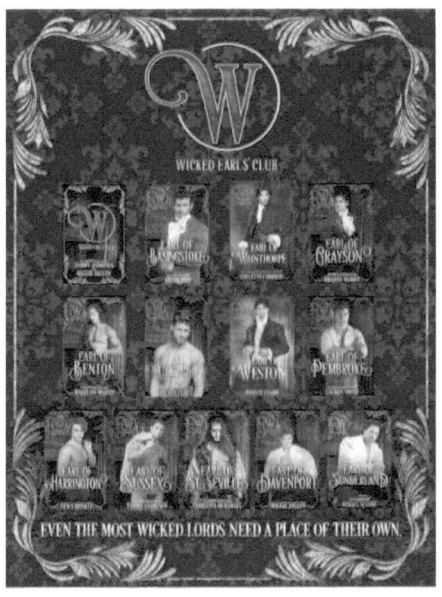

Meet twelve of the most wickedly sinful earls in all of Regency England. Together they make up the Wicked Earls' Club. A secret group, marked with a single golden W; it is a place where these deliciously devious earls can indulge in their darkest desires. Though fate may have something else planned for them entirely. Read twelve standalone novellas as each wicked earl finds love and redemption.

AUTHOR'S NOTES

I'd love to hear from you!
You can contact me at:
Christina@christinamcknight.com

Or write me at:
P.O. Box 1017
Patterson, CA 95363

www.ChristinaMcKnight.com
Check out my website for giveaways, book reviews, and
information on my upcoming projects,
or connect with me through social media at:
Twitter: @CMcKnightWriter
Facebook: www.facebook.com/christinamcknightwriter
Goodreads: www.goodreads.com/ChristinaMcKnight

Sign up for my newsletter here:
http://eepurl.com/VP1rP

Turn the page for an excerpt from
The Thief Steals Her Earl,
Book 1 in the Craven House Series!

The Thief Steals Her Earl
Now available

TO SAVE HER FAMILY, SHE MUST BE VERY, VERY BAD...

Miss Judith Pengarden has a problem: her family is in debt, and soon will lose their home. What's a dutiful sister to do to save her loved ones from ruination? Why, steal a few items from an aristocrat's house--items he'll surely never miss--and sell them to pay her family's debts. Luckily for her, she meets Simon Montgomery, the new Earl of Cartwright, a recluse familiar with antiquities. He can help her keep her family from debtor's prison, and he might just claim her heart too. Except instead of stealing from Simon's neighbor, she breaks into the wrong house...

Simon is determined to change the way the world sees his family, even if it means he can no longer pursue his dreams of being a scholar to take on his new title. When a thief breaks into his home and steals a precious family heirloom, he vows to get the item back. The last thing he expects is that the girl he met at a garden party is a thief! When Jude is discovered with his possessions, how will she ever convince him that despite her deception, her love for him is the truth?

London, England
May 1818

JUDE PLUCKED AT the sturdy wool of her filth-
streaked pinafore as she held her breath to keep the
wretched smells at bay. The stink of unwashed bodies,
moldy, forgotten food, and wet animal was
overpowered only by the stench of a coppery odor she
knew to be spilled blood. She'd certainly need to burn
her current garment as soon as she was released and
able to return to Craven House—if one of her siblings
ever saw fit to collect her.

To do away with such a precious thing as a dress was not something she'd always had the liberty to do. For many years, she counted herself lucky to possess several dresses—even though she shared each with Samantha. The time she and her siblings had spent at Craven House should have prepared Jude for this night; men angered by too much drink, which turned into arguing, which led to fisticuffs and blood—the smell of which was something she'd never forget, though her family had tried to keep her far from it as much as possible.

A sliver of the rising sun outside the narrow window of her cell allowed a slice of light to penetrate her dank enclosure; though Jude would have been happy to remain ignorant of her despicable surroundings. Her dress, though made from a thick material, still snagged on the rough, splintering bench below her. But after hours of standing—and pacing— Jude had to rest her aching legs. It was either the sticky, grimy, wooden bench or the more intolerable hard-packed dirt floor littered with discarded food and a pail filled with what she was told was water but appeared murkier than the River Thames.

Actually, she'd prefer a swim in the Thames as opposed to her current predicament. She only hoped her elder brother, Garrett, didn't ship her to the country for all the trouble she'd caused. The trouble she presumed herself in. A sojourn to the country would be preferable to what Marce, her imperious sister, would do to her if she found out about Jude's escapades.

She'd seen herself as invincible; above being caught—so much so that Jude should be in a complete panic. But the surreal nature of her position hadn't faded to allow in the stark actuality she faced.

It was supposed to be only once—the vase from Lord Gunther's townhouse. They were to sell the piece, give the money to Marce, and be free to live with some semblance of peace knowing their home was safe. But the vase remained at Craven House and now their family's future was in jeopardy. They should have known that a stolen vase would not go unnoticed and unreported in the post. They should not have been so delusional as to think they could take the vase and gain coin for it as easily as selling wares inside the marketplace.

As of now, she'd been left unaccompanied in this darkened room, the door securely locked, for hours. No one had come to inquire about her well-being; no offers of refreshment or fare, no blanket to ward off the night chill. She hadn't heard another person since the constable had slammed the door shut on her with his sharp reprimand to not cause him further grievance or he'd make her sorry.

She was unsure how much longer she'd be locked in this room—her stomach let out a loud growl in protest at the thought—or even if her twin, Samantha, knew where she'd been taken.

One thing Jude was certain of; she didn't relish spending another moment alone here. The window was too narrow for her to wiggle through and the door was bolted from the outside.

This led her to hours of pondering how she'd ended up here—what path she could have taken to deliver herself from such a wretched circumstance.

Her night had started off simple enough, with she and her twin devising a plan to remove fourteenth century Bible leaves from Lord Asherton's townhouse—a far less notable and traceable antiquity than the vase from Lord Gunther, but almost as valuable. It should have been easy. Samantha was to meet the lord in question at a dinner party she was attending with friends while Jude slipped into his home, collected the ancient papers, and disappeared as if she'd never been there. They'd heard during a recent outing that the man's house was light on servants as many had traveled to Lord Asherton's country estate ahead of his scheduled departure on the morrow. The perfect time for their heist.

But little had gone as planned.

After searching a study on the ground floor, Jude had fled down a dark hallway when she'd heard voices coming from the kitchen, growing louder as she rushed in the opposite direction. It hadn't been difficult to slip into an empty room, rush to a door, and flee—that was until her cap was ripped from her head as she bolted by a coat rack positioned inside what appeared to be a lady's sitting room. Jude had quickly retrieved the cap, tugged it back into place to hide her red hair, and continued toward a door she hoped would open to a garden sitting area...and her freedom.

She was mere steps from the door when the alarm sounded behind her.

Not the shouts of an infuriated lord or the call to halt by a faithful servant, but rather the searing shriek of a child. Jude barely glanced over her shoulder to see her identifier before rushing through the door, along the side of the house, and around to the narrow lane behind the row of townhouses.

Several hours later, her ears still rung from the high-pitched screech.

She would never forget the rounded, frightened eyes of the young girl who'd peered at Jude from her seat on the lounge, a throw blanket lying haphazardly across her lap as she read a book. Her tousled hair fell around her shoulders, still crimped from her plaits. A pristine white night shift gathered at her throat in a bow.

Jude couldn't accurately describe the girl beyond her long, dark hair and frightened look.

All she'd thought about at that moment was getting as far away from Lord Asherton's home as possible, the valuable Bible leaves be damned.

Fleeing from the house and gaining a block's distance hadn't stopped an alarm being sounded. The night watchman was rushing around the corner, his lamp held high to illuminate his way.

The burly man, dressed in merchant's trousers and coat, was only identifiable by the shiny tin star pinned to his jacket pocket. The swinging lamp sent light reflecting off the dinted piece of metal as they both stood stock-still, staring at one another. The pair was caught in the small circle of light given off by the uplighter. His expression was likely a mirror image of hers; fright.

She hadn't expected to be caught and it was probable he had never apprehended a suspected criminal on his nightly watch.

She was an unchaperoned woman, dressed in a less than fashionable gown with a cap hiding her hair. It was reasonable for the constable to question her on principle alone, for what woman would be traversing the deserted London streets at close to midnight?

Maybe she should have run. Sam would have vouched for this course of action.

Certainly, she should not have agreed to the harebrained notion in the first place. Marce would have counseled against it.

The man wasn't armed. Most night watchmen took to their route with nothing more than a billy club as protection.

And so, the standoff continued. Jude was analyzing the watchman's size and strength; concluding he would easily outrun her on foot in a section of London she was unfamiliar with.

There'd been little else for her to do but employ her twin's claimed talent for charming men. Unfortunately, her voice didn't hold the sultry depth of Sam's, nor was Jude adept at the coy behavior needed to lull a man into feeling secure enough to allow his guard to fall.

And so, she'd relented and allowed the watchman to lock her in this room—as any criminal would deserve.

Jude gave in to her exhaustion and leaned back against the grimy wall, needing to forget her many mistakes. She settled against the cold wall of her locked cell and drew her knees to her chest, allowing her dress to cover her chilled feet. As her head met the hard surface of the stone, she closed her eyes, begging her tears to stay where they belonged, unshed.

She would not cry. That right had been taken from her when she and her twin had decided to help bring extra income to Craven House—they'd known the risk they'd agreed to take with their actions.

She breathed deeply, allowing the stench of her surroundings to invade her nostrils and then expelled gradually, slowing her pulse. If she could calm herself, maybe sleep would take over and she'd wake to find it had all been an unpleasant nightmare. She'd awaken in her warm bed with Sam nestled in her matching one a few feet away, both tucked deeply under their soft, peach eyelet, down blankets. Jude would share her horrid dream with Sam. They'd laugh as they crawled from the warmth of their well-sprung beds and rang for their maid to help them prepare for their day of shopping and entertainments.

Except, Sam and Jude shared one bed, hadn't the luxury of a maid, nor the spare funds for as much as even a new pair of gloves.

Marce reminded her younger sisters, daily, each time they offered their complaints, that many women were much less fortunate than they. At least they had a roof over their heads, food in their pantry, and some hope for a more fruitful future if they minded their behavior and attracted fine suitors.

And they had love.

They undoubtedly had an abundance of love.

But love would not keep the debt collectors at bay, nor garner additional food for their table.

And a new dress or two for them all would be appreciated, especially since Lady Haversham had been so kind as to sponsor their societal debut.

Jude huffed. It was a trivial, selfish thought, especially when she was perched on a splintered bench with her head leaning against a grime-covered wall in a room that hadn't been properly swept in Lord knew how long.

From somewhere outside the cell, Jude heard loud, angry voices. They were muffled by the wall and door separating her from other parts of the building housing her, but the aggression in the dominant voice was unmistakable.

Jude would prefer a large hole open in the room and swallow her, as opposed to the force of nature currently headed her way. Only moments would pass before the ire presently unleashed on the night watchman who dared keep Miss Judith Pengarden locked in a room, would be refocused on Jude herself.

"I will not stand for this, Garrett," Marce, Jude's eldest sister and only motherly figure, bit out harshly as a key was slid into the lock. "I will have this door opened at once or I will bring the fires of Hades down on this *establishment.*" Marce's emphasis on the word left no doubt in anyone's mind what her family's matriarch thought of the night watchman and his lodgings.

"Dear sister," Garrett coaxed. "The man is only doing his job, earning a respectable salary while keeping the night streets free of vagabonds."

"Judith is most certainly not a vagabond." Marce's voice rose three octaves until it was almost a shrill scream. "Now, release her at once or I will be forced to call on Lord Haversham or Lord Chastain. I am certain you know both the earl and the duke. They will quickly settle all this once and for all."

Jude could picture her sister stamping her foot, her fury intensifying with each word.

No one dared defy Marce—not at Craven House or anywhere else she'd witnessed her sister in action.

"Ma'am," the night watchman stammered, clearly

resigned to following Marce's orders. "My apologies for the mistake. The alarm was sounded and the butler in the household gave a description matching Miss Judith's appearance."

"And when you found nothing incriminating on her person, you decided the best course of action was to lock her up for hours in this flea-infested room? Most certainly not proper accommodations for a woman of her status."

"Calm yourself, Marce." Garrett attempted to soothe his sister's wrath. "I know Mr. Newman would not purposely apprehend an innocent young woman."

"I can assure you it was not—" Newman tried unsuccessfully to interject.

"I will not calm down." The door was wrenched open, its hinges groaning in protest at the swift movement. "If one hair on her head is harmed, I will have *you* drawn and quartered!"

Marce, her blonde hair falling down her back unrestrained and her coat buttoned down her front, stormed into the room with Garrett close on her heels. The night watchman remained outside, likely knowing it's safer for him to stay out of Jude's eldest sister's reach.

"Again," said Mr. Newman. "I was also worried about her being out late at night. She could have been set upon by any sort of unsavory character. She was without a chaperone and was unwilling to give me any information about herself beyond your direction, Lord Garrett."

Jude would have laughed at the use of Garrett's name spoken so formally, but that would draw Marce's attention far sooner than Jude was prepared for.

Her sister may be vehemently protective of her siblings, but that in no way meant she coddled them.

"That will be all, Mr. Newman." Retreating footsteps sounded as the poor man heeded Marce's curt dismissal. But with his retreating steps, Marce's concern also fled. "What exactly were you doing wandering London at midnight?"

Jude knew better than to speak. It was a rhetorical question meant to keep her silent, for Marce was in no way finished talking.

"I can tell you where you were *not* last night. You were not attending the Buckhams' soiree with Lady Haversham and Mrs. Jakeston, as you should have been. You also did not arrive home with Samantha. I dare say you did not so much as depart with your twin at the start of your evening." Marce's brow rose, daring Jude to refute her. "What do you have to say for yourself, Judith Pengarden?"

Marce only used the siblings' full names when trouble was afoot and she knew it could tarnish their family—as much as their scandal-ridden clan could be tarnished where they hung on the fringes of London's proper *ton*.

"Is there something you'd like to hear from me?" Jude retorted, any calm she may have achieved disappearing.

It irked Jude to no end that Marce viewed her as a mere child—always the girl in plaits and kid boots—not a mature, educated woman, old enough by society's standards to marry and start her own home and family. However, here Jude sat: in a dank room when any proper lady should be abed, accused of stealing into the home of a member of the *beau monde*.

And all because she was attempting to help her family.

Garrett stepped between his sisters. "I beg the both of you, finish this conversation in a less public," he paused, looking at the filth overtaking the room, as if seeing it for the first time, "and certainly more hygienic, place. After Jude is allowed a hot—very hot—bath to cleanse this awful stink from her."

Mockingly, he brought a loose tendril of her hair to his nose and sniffed, disgust masking his teasing nature.

She swatted at his hand and allowed her curl to fall from his grasp.

Jude looked to her sister, silently pleading for Marce to take Garrett's suggestion.

Marce's narrowed stare said she wasn't convinced they need move their conversation. "I have a mind to leave you here."

"Leave me here?" Jude gulped.

"Leave her here?" Garrett said at the same time.

"Why not?" Marce set her hand on her hip as she stepped around her younger brother to face Jude once more. "I am unsure what you—and likely Sam—are up to, but I will not allow you to run about London with no regard for the consequences. Both for you and our family as a whole."

"I despise when you speak rationally." Jude crossed her arms and stood, signaling her desire to depart. "It would be best to return home before we are spotted leaving a place of such ill repute."

"Thank you for thinking of someone and something other than your own pleasures," Marce said before turning on her heels and leaving the room with as much fanfare as she'd entered it. She left Garrett and Jude staring blankly at one another. "Come along, you two."

The comment stung, but the truth in Marce's words was undeniable. Her sister may not admit when she needed help, but Jude's actions were risky and not as thought out as she'd hoped. It was highly likely Jude would never be adept at such things. Thankfully, she had no interest in repeating her actions. Not until their financial situation became increasingly dire, at least.

She vowed to refocus on being rid of the vase and not entangling herself in any more harrowing escapades about London.

"I have no doubt your reasoning for tarrying about after the midnight hour is very compelling, yet less than savory." Garrett took Jude's elbow and guided her from the dirty room, both of them squeezing through the doorway. "Sam's note of warning did not find me abed either." He winked with his words, letting Jude know he was concerned about her but would not pry—as he loathed his siblings prying into his affairs.

Jude turned rounded eyes on her elder brother— the lone wolf of a family full of females. She'd often wondered what occupied his many leisurely hours, but her need to respect his privacy outweighed her interest.

"Do not dally." Marce's call floated down the long corridor leading to the front of the establishment, her sure footsteps keeping time. "I have no qualms about leaving the pair of you to secure your own transport home."

Jude allowed Garrett to walk her down the hall as she suppressed a sigh at her sister's ire.

The situation seemed drastically less dreadful now that she was among the free again.

She and Garrett nodded to the watchman as they crossed the threshold into the cool morning air. A little bird chirped in the tree bordering the front walk.

"You will owe her answers when you arrive home," Garrett confided.

"I am aware."

"I hope you have thought up a plausible explanation in your hours spent locked down."

"I have not," Jude said.

Both remained quiet as a man came down the path before them. The stranger removed his hat and nodded to Marce in greeting. If her sister issued any response, it was too quiet for Jude to hear.

"Good morn," the man greeted Jude and Garrett, a grim smile on his face as he looked away. His hair fell across his forehead at the movement, but he quickly brushed it aside. As he did, Jude noticed the youthfulness of his face.

She glanced over her shoulder as the man pushed his spectacles farther onto the bridge of his nose and strode into the night watchman's home, his trousers and coat wrinkled as if he'd either slept in them or was against bothering his valet this early in the day.

"And to you, good sir," Garrett called as the door closed behind the man, her brother's shoulders lifting as he steered Jude toward their waiting carriage. It was very much like Garrett to puff his chest when faced with a gentleman of peerage, something he longed to be but had given up on years before—the forgotten younger son of a deceased lord.

Garrett's horse stood tethered to a post nearby.

Jude's heart sank. "You will not return to Craven House with us?"

"I fear not, mop," he said, handing her up into the carriage where Marce was already arranging her skirts. "I have much to attend to."

Marce chuckled softly from inside. "I'm certain he does."

He turned a peeved look at their eldest sister inside the dim conveyance before continuing, "However, I will be round this afternoon to discuss…things."

Jude hoped they could discuss "things" without her present, for she was certain she would be excluded from any and all talks of punishment due her.

"I shall be canceling my trip," Marce said when Jude seated herself across from her. "There is something afoot and I will not let this family go to ruins in my absence."

There was certainly something happening, but it was far more concerning than Sam's and Jude's antics.

"It is one week, Marce." Garrett entered the carriage, his own transport forgotten as he motioned Jude to scoot over and allow him room to sit.

Their sister left her siblings for only one short week every year. Sometimes it was immediately following the holiday season, other times it was during the summer months, but she always returned a bit lighter in nature. They'd come to relish the short time Marce was gone, never asking her destination. But Payton—Jude's youngest sister—had assumed for years that Marce traveled to Bath for several days of rest before returning to her obligations. Jude's sisters envied Marce's travels, thinking they were excluded from something enjoyable, but Jude could only imagine the weight on her sister's shoulders. She cared for so many—receiving nothing in return. If she sought a few days to live a normal, carefree life then Jude could not blame her for taking it.

Many days, Jude wished she had the fortitude to do the same.

Take her life and future into her own hands, provide for herself instead of partaking in what Marce worked tirelessly to provide for them. Instead, she'd been told continually that at her tender age, she was still to be taken care of. Far too young and innocent to take on any further responsibilities.

And that had led to finding another way around Marce's ban on Jude being anything more than a debutante—protected, sheltered, and treated as a delicate thing.

A way to help support their large household and push the debt collectors back. One time. That was to be the end of it, but when they'd been unable to sell the stolen vase, they'd had to alter their plans slightly, which included Jude taking the Bible leaves.

Another failure and setback for them.

"I can handle things at Craven House in your absence."

Garrett's declaration snapped Jude back to the present.

"That is not necessary," Jude snapped. "We are of an age to care for ourselves."

"In a fashion similar to last night?" Marce asked. "I think not."

"Then it is settled—" Garrett started.

"Nothing is settled," Marce refuted, turning a sharp look on the pair. "I no more trust you to keep Craven

House from burning to the ground than I trust the twins. It's bloody insane, but I think Payton has a better handle on herself than the lot of you."

"Payton?" Jude and Garrett said at the same time, once again.

"Do stop doing that," Jude hissed at her brother. "People will think you and I are more closely related than Samantha and me."

"Is that so awful?" he teased. "I am undoubtedly more attractive than she."

"We look identical, you cad!" Jude felt her temper rising as it did on most occasions when she and Garrett were in the same place.

"Then I will be the pretty twin." Garrett fluttered his eyes, his long lashes being one of his most notable features—if not as manly as he'd like. "I am certain to have many offers for my hand. Our dear eldest sister will be fighting off my hungry suitors!"

Jude swatted at him and he hurriedly scooted out of her reach on the bench seat, fluttering his hand as if fanning the heat from his face.

His actions were at odds with his purely masculine, deep chuckle at his lark.

It only took a moment for her annoyance to fade and a smile to appear.

He jested with Jude constantly. She should feel honored to have their only brother's undivided attention so regularly when he rarely noticed Payton or Sam, but that also meant he kept better watch over her.

He loved his sisters, but Jude especially. Though he was a man about town, he never went long without visiting Craven House, no matter how often Marce insisted she did not need his concern over their well-being.

"You two will certainly send me to an early grave with your mischief," Marce declared, her voice thin with exhaustion.

The trio settled into a companionable silence as

their carriage traversed the bustling morning streets. A footman followed with Garrett's mount. Each was lost to their own musings as the carriage found its way quickly home.

Mr. Curtis opened the carriage door with a flourish befitting a man half his age.

"M'lady." He bowed to Marce as she exited, his back creaking with his effort. "This missive came for ye when ye was out."

"Not another one," Jude heard Marce mumble. "This has to stop."

"You will rectify this shortly, will you not?" Garrett asked as he stepped down and turned to assist Jude. But she rebuffed his assistance and he turned back to Marce. "I do hope this is the last time."

"For all of our futures, I certainly hope so."

Jude hopped down from the carriage, snapping a quick glance at the letter before it disappeared into the folds of her sister's gown. The envelope was labeled as clearly as the others Jude had seen: *Notice: Delinquency—Funds Due!*

She couldn't help but feel she'd been privy to a conversation that was not meant for her ears.

In that instant, Jude regretted her decisions for the night, yet at the same time, knew the ends justified the means. She must remember she was, indeed, helping Marce and everyone who called Craven House their home. Though she needed to focus more on not getting caught if her great measures were to help and not hinder everything her family had worked so hard for.

Available in print, audiobook, and e-book now!

ABOUT THE AUTHOR

USA TODAY Bestselling Author Christina McKnight writes emotional and intricate Regency Romance with strong women and maverick heroes.

Her books combine romance and mystery, exploring themes of redemption and forgiveness. When she's not writing, Christina enjoys trying new coffeehouses, visiting wine bars, traveling the world, and watching television.

Email: Christina@ChristinaMcKnight.com
Follow her on Twitter: @CMcKnightWriter
Keep up to date on her releases:
www.christinamcknight.com
Like Christina's FB Author page:
ChristinaMcKnightWriter

www.ingramcontent.com/pod-product-compliance
Lightning Source LLC
Chambersburg PA
CBHW021231130626
46554CB00004B/1431